A Night of Wickedness

JD Nelson

To Nels, always Nels

THIRD TIME'S A CHARM
KORRINA

"Korrina Manetas?"

"That's me," I replied, giving the bailiff a little wave with my fingers. I couldn't move much with my handcuffs attached to the shackles on my ankles.

"Would you please step inside?" he asked, waiting until I passed by him before he followed me inside the courtroom and closed the door.

I held my breath as eyes, every color of the spectrum, trained on me as I walked through the quiet courtroom, passed the benches, and took my place in front of the judge. I was a little relieved to see that there were some sad eyes among them, but it was no surprise that most were squinted in contempt. They knew guilty when they saw it.

After shuffling through a pile of papers, the judge looked up and said, "Korrina Manetas, you were arrested on April twenty-ninth by Captain Leon Patras of the Bureau and have been charged with public indecency. Were you not warned about the consequences of a repeat offense the last time you were in this courtroom?"

"Yes, your honor, but..."

"But what? You were caught having sexual intercourse behind the Starbucks with a young satyr by the name of ..." He looked through another stack of papers and extracted one. "Here it is— Agapios. Is he present?"

A silky, accented voice sounded from my left. "ναι, εγώ είμαι εδώ."

"English please, Agapios."

1

"Yes. I am here, your honor."

"I trust that I will not find you back in this courtroom after this."

"No, indeed. When Korrina is in prison, I will no longer have a reason to engage a woman out of doors."

The entire room erupted into laughter around me. If I could have sunk through the floor, I would have done it the second Agapios finished speaking. How could this day be any worse? Or embarrassing?

The judge banged the gavel twice, and the crowd quieted down to whispers. "Miss Manetas, how do you plead?"

"Guilty," I answered, not even bothering to look him in the eyes. I knew him well enough to know exactly the look I was getting right now.

"My dear, I have known you since you were a youngling on your mother's hip. You have always been a sweet, thoughtful child. We all know that here." He gave a hard look to the naysayers in the crowd. "But you know this community is a haven for our kind. If a human had spotted you, you could have put Meadowbrook in a spotlight that we can't afford to be under. Do you understand?"

I didn't understand anything. Everyone in Meadowbrook knew that it was almost impossible for a nymph to control their sexual side. Most were nymphs themselves, for Pete's sake. They had the same cravings, the same temptations I had. I mean, it wasn't as if everyone else in the courtroom wasn't doing the exact same thing. The only difference between the others and I was that they had somewhere to take their lovers. I had nowhere. With fifteen brothers and sisters still living at home, I had zero privacy. Not to mention the two nagging parents who refused to let me move out ... though I'm already twenty-eight, make enough to support myself at the Piggly Wiggly, and was slowly losing my friggin' mind.

Ordinary people, desperate for sex, would just do it in the

woods, away from prying eyes. I couldn't do that, either. Thousands of trees would relay a play by play to anyone who would listen if I did.

Ugh. Being a nymph sucks. Don't let anyone tell you otherwise.

"Korrina? I'm waiting," the judge prompted.

"Yes, your honor. I understand."

"Do you have anything to say for yourself before I read your sentence?"

"Only that I am sorry, Uncle Solon. I meant to do better this time."

He nodded in that solemn way of his, and I knew life as I knew it was over. My uncle adhered to the law, no matter what the circumstances were. He wouldn't let our connection stop him from sending me to the Bureau's prison, favorite niece or not. Justice was always served in his courtroom. He was notorious for it.

"I know you did your best, Korrina. I fear that it is your parents, and even I, that have failed in this. You have only done what it is in your nature to do." He paused as if reluctant to continue. "Korrina Manetas, this court finds you guilty of the charges laid upon you. In light of your exemplary community service records, and because we all understand the struggles that you're going through, the court has determined that prison would be too harsh of a punishment. You will, instead, leave Meadowbrook to serve your sentence in a little populated, rural community in southern Alabama. There you will remain for five years. If in five years you have kept out of trouble, and if you have not been incarcerated for any other crimes, we will welcome you back to Meadowbrook with open arms."

Tears slipped down my cheeks. They wanted me to leave the only home I'd ever known? Even if I didn't have many friends here or my own place to live, one lousy night of wickedness would never be worth losing everything I worked so hard for, especially the thirty-second tryst with Agapios. Looking back, I couldn't believe that I'd broken my probation for him at all. He'd never been particularly handsome or witty. Hell, he'd never even been nice. Damn these insatiable urges of mine! They were never anything but a pain in my magical ass.

My uncle sighed heavily and continued, "I do ask that you try to stay out of trouble. The Bureau authorities outside of our town will not be as lenient as I am. Settle down with a nice human or a preternatural creature of some sort. It matters little, but you must stay out of trouble."

"Yes, sir. I promise."

"Take the morning to say your goodbyes and pack. You leave tonight for your new home." He looked past me and sneered when he saw the smug smile my partner in crime wore. "Agapios, your sentencing is next. And don't you go thinking that you will get a slap on the wrist for your involvement in this. This is your third offense as well."

***

A million tears, goodbyes, and miles later, I pulled down the oak-lined driveway that would take me to my new sanctuary. The satellite view on the Google Maps page did not do the house justice. From the ground, it was beyond anything I could've expected. In awe, I sat in my car and just stared at it in amazement.

The house was in the Greek revival style, with two huge white columns that stood proudly on either side of red-painted double doors. A long balcony was situated above, overlooking the expanse of the acreage. Without my family around me, I'd have to rely on the flora for strength, so I really hoped the balcony would be accessible from my room. If it wasn't, I guess I could make whatever room it was in into my bedroom. I did have the run of the place.

I smiled to myself. Could Uncle Solon have calculated my punishment to get me out from under the oppressive thumb of my father? Most definitely, he could have. In addition, he knew I'd always wanted to live in a historic home, and this antebellum would fit that bill quite nicely. Solon wasn't my favorite uncle for nothing. He was smart, fair, and he listened when I spoke, unlike everyone else in the nymph community.

Giddy at the turn of circumstances, I got out of the car and immediately started searching for the key. Just as promised, I found it under the flower pot next to the front doors. Perhaps not the best hiding spot, however, it was unlikely that anyone else would try to use the key. My nearest neighbor, Mr. Raines, was a half mile away through the woods, and the rest of the surrounding area was undeveloped land owned by Oswin Enterprises, a regional development firm. I'd probably never see anyone around here—ever. That was the punishment part that I'd been waiting on. Solon knew that I hated solitude, and he'd given me five years of it. Damn, he was good. He was sneaky as hell but good.

Unfortunately, getting into my new house was not as easy as just turning the key. I had to ram the pollen-covered door with my shoulder to get it to budge. Finally, after the third bone-rattling blow, it opened with a loud pop. A quick examination determined that it had been stuck with what would probably turn out to be fifty years of grime and mildew. Gross.

My first glance at the inside of the house was as discouraging as the door had been. It was insanely filthy from floor to ceiling. Someone had the presence of mind to cover the furniture with what I assumed used to be thick white sheets, but I didn't hold any hope what was underneath hadn't molded and rotted away with the humidity Alabama was famous for.

Lifting the closest sheet, I was surprised to find a deep blue settee in near perfect condition. Excited at the discovery, I carefully rolled back the rest of the sheet to reveal the beautiful sofa's hand carved legs and back. If the other furniture had been kept in excellent condition like this, we were in business.

I looked around. There was no sense in uncovering anything else before I went to the store for cleaning supplies. Taking care of this criminally dirty house would have to come first.

VAMPIRES CAN SUCK IT
KORRINA

October 1st

My dream house is becoming a nightmare. How could one house be so dirty? Didn't the owner have any pride in this grand old house? I've had to go back so many times for cleaning supplies, Mr. Greene at the general store is starting to think I have OCD.

Honestly, I should've asked my uncle to send me to the Bureau's prison. At least, I'd still have the long fingernails I arrived with, instead of the nubs I have now.

Wish me luck, journal. I tackle the kitchen today, and I'm pretty sure lizards are living in the sink.

K

I think the key to feeling at home in any new place is making it your own. After the clean-a-thon, moving furniture, and unpacking boxes for three days straight, I could barely wiggle my fingers, but I was happier than I'd been in a long time. The house was beginning to feel something like home. And as an added bonus, with every wipe of a banister or sweep I made with the broom, I uncovered my new home's real beauty.

The only downfall of surrounding oneself in all the splendor was that I kept catching myself daydreaming. Maybe it was the isolation getting to me, but I kept imagining all the dances they might have had in the ballroom. I dreamt of all the kisses those ball goers might have stolen underneath the gazebo in the backyard. Not to mention, all of the ensuing passionate nights spent in the ornate four-poster beds that were sequestered by the heaviest curtains I'd ever had the misfortune of dry cleaning.

Yep, one thing was for sure. Either I needed someone to talk to, or I was high from the fumes of the bleach cleaner. Which one? I had no idea. With my overbearing parents and twenty-seven brothers and sisters, I'd never been alone this long in my life.

***

After the third long day of cleaning, I rolled out of bed feeling like I'd spent the night before filling in for a rodeo clown. Every muscle in my body was as limp as a noodle, and my long dark hair was a rat's nest. Despite that, I planned on spending the afternoon getting the backyard in shape. The trellis the wisteria grew on was nearly bowed to the ground with all the overgrowth weighing it down.

Dragging myself out of bed, I managed to work up the energy to put on clothes and brush my hair then stepped out onto the back porch. What I found out there nearly bought me to my knees with desire. There was a landscaping truck parked in the driveway and several men already at work—several shirtless, tan, hard-bodied men.

Whoa.

The nymph in me had my heart pounding with excitement. She knew exactly what these men could offer her and was chomping at the bit to introduce herself. But the sane, reasonable part of me knew that I couldn't take advantage of this fortuitous answer to my loneliness, no matter how much I desperately wanted to. I'd promised Solon I could control my urges, and I would do just that. Even if it killed me to walk away from something so deliciously available.

With my mouth set in a grim line, I balanced my gardening gloves on the porch railing and ducked low in the back yard's high grass. What else could I do? If they spotted me, it was all over. I wouldn't be able to ignore them, and it was highly doubtful they'd be able to ignore me. I streaked forward to the safety of the trees and brush with a burst of speed. From there, I aimed myself east and didn't stop running until I could breathe without raw need punctuating every breath I took.

Looking around, it was apparent the trees knew I had moved into the house. They were all tilted, with their reaching branches angled toward where I slept. I trailed my fingers along the trunk of an old oak as I walked by and felt a sort of magical high five from the tree. They were excited to see me—like a puppy is when you get home from a long day at work.

"Hello," I said. "I'm Korrina Manetas from Meadowbrook."

In unison, the elder trees of the grove spoke aloud. "Welcome, child. We have been awaiting your arrival."

Surprised, I asked, "You knew I was coming to Goshen?"

"Word travels fast within the forest."

I sighed. That wasn't embarrassing or anything. Nothing like being judged by a thousand trees at one time.

"Worry not, Korrina. We care nothing for circumstances of your arrival. Indeed, we do not care for the present-day laws of humans. You act as nature has intended."

I gaped at the trees. The citizens of Meadowbrook didn't give me this kind of support during my trial, and they had known me all of my life! "Thank you," I told them. It felt good to have someone on my side if only so I didn't feel like an asshole for all the righteous indignation I'd been feeling since my departure from all decent society. Once the novelty of living on my own had passed, I felt a little peeved that my uncle had made an example out of me.

***

I spoke with the trees for the better part of an hour, getting to know them and letting them get to know me. It was a real treat to speak to them out loud, instead of telepathically. In Meadowbrook, the trees never deigned us worthy of their ethereal, lilting voices. Probably because of the way nymphs used them there. They weren't revered the way they were long ago. Now they were relegated to being instruments used to give a nymph a pick-me-up or to spread gossip. I had always thought that to be an enormous waste. When you could become one with nature, you should appreciate the gift, not exploit it.

I decided to keep exploring the woods after I said my goodbyes to the grove. Besides the occasional snake, fox, and bobcat, I didn't see much along my trek until I stumbled upon my neighbor's house, which was an exact replica of my house. It was obvious the two were built together sometime in the eighteen hundreds. In all appearances, the house seemed to be vacant, but I knew better. Someone was alive in there. Well, maybe alive wasn't the right word. Undead would be a much more accurate description.

Holy crap. Mr. Raines was a vampire.

Vampires were a cursed lot. They were cursed to darkness, to blood drinking, and eventually, to having a stake thrust through their hearts. It's not that I have anything against them. That's just the way it was. The peacekeepers for the Bureau were notorious for dusting a vampire before hearing their side of any story.

Dead human + Fang marks = Immediate death by tree limb.

Fear raced through me as I crept up to the window closest to me and peered inside the dusty glass. Mr. Raines had either just moved in a few days ago or he didn't intend to clean the house ever again. It was a disgrace. All the elegant furnishings and crystal chandeliers drooped from the weight of the dust accumulated on them. Making a sound of disgust, I turned away and started on my trip back home. The vampire owed it to the house to make it as beautiful as it once had been. Maybe, I could convince him to hire an extremely bored nymph to clean his place up, or perhaps, he'd rip my throat out. It was a coin toss.

Thankfully, the yard crew was gone when I returned to the house. I breathed a huge sigh of relief and let myself into the back door. It was full dark now, and honestly, the vampire next door had me a little spooked. With his keen senses, he had to know I lived here by now. That knowledge made me uneasy as hell. I just wanted to lock the doors and sink into a hot bath with a shot of whiskey to soothe my jangled nerves.

"Were you looking for me at my house?" A silky voice asked from the shadow of the refrigerator.

Terrified, I shrieked and lunged for the light switch. I didn't have the luxury of having night vision like Mr. Raines did. I needed to see what I was up against. And possibly find a makeshift weapon.

As if he was used to the reaction I gave, my unfazed vampire neighbor stepped out into the full light of the kitchen and smiled at me. I sucked in a breath as my body instantly flushed with lust. He was tall, very tall, with thick dark hair, the strangest amber eyes I'd ever seen, and a face that was made for the runway. In other words, he was absolutely resplendent. And might I add, ridiculously tempting for a potential killer.

"Calm yourself, Miss Manetas," he said gently. "I truly did not mean to startle you."

Super relieved he'd mistaken my accelerated heartbeat for fear, I tentatively returned his smile. "How do you know who I am?"

His all-encompassing stare did not waver as he slowly reached into his coat and pulled out a letter. "I received your mail by mistake."

I looked down and saw the Alabama Power Company's logo on the letter. "Thanks," I said, moving forward to snatch it out of his hand before I quickly backed myself up against the door again.

Mr. Raines frowned, his friendly demeanor now nowhere to be found. "You know, Korrina, for an immortal, you are very rude."

My mouth dropped open. "You think I'm rude?" I asked. "I'm not the one who broke into someone's house to scare the life out of them!"

He straightened his tie and spoke down to me in a disdainful, frosty voice that set my teeth on edge. "No, I suppose not. You did, however, peer into my windows like a peeping Tom. Have you no decency at all?" He paused and gave a cruel little laugh. "No. How silly of me. Of course, you don't. You're a nymph."

As much as his words stung, he had me there. I did peep into his windows. "I-I thought the house was vacant," I stammered, trying to find a way to backtrack out of this situation. I couldn't afford to get into trouble so soon after my banishment.

"Liar."

"You know what? Get the fuck out of my house," I told him, my temper spiking. Vampire or not, no one was going to speak to me like that in my own home.

"Very well," he seethed, his voice positively dripping with hatred. "Good evening, Miss Manetas.

I didn't return his farewell. I only stared after him in horror. What had I just done?

***

I waited hours for the panic to subside after Mr. Raines left. It didn't. I was still wholly terrified he would go to the Bureau and tell them how I'd been conducting myself only four days after I arrived. I even considered apologizing (which should tell you how desperate I was), but I didn't. I had too much pride for that, especially after he snuck into my house and scared the bejeezus out of me for no reason. He would have to apologize for that mean trick before I ever said I was sorry to him. On that, I would not budge.

That resolve and bravado lasted, maybe, twenty more minutes. When I heard the grandfather clock strike four, I couldn't stand it anymore. I locked up the door and set out through the woods to walk to his house. If he didn't forgive me—fine—but I had to know what he intended to do.

I found Mr. Raines standing on his porch, admiring the full moon. His keen eyes darted to me, tracking me as I walked across the yard and stepped up the stairs to face him. There was a tiny amount of hope left in my heart that he would ignore what I did, and I was clinging onto it with all my might.

"Good morning, Mr. Raines," I said, smiling a little too brightly. He looked like he was in a more pleasant mood. Maybe he was just hungry when he was cranky earlier?

He returned my smile with a serene one of his own. "Good morning, Miss Manetas."

"H-how are you?" I stuttered. I was a little distracted by how insanely sexy he was. I had to wonder if that was his natural allure or if I was just really horny. Sometimes it was hard to tell. And, honestly, it was probably a bit of both.

Okay, definitely a bit of both.

"I am well," he answered cordially. "And yourself?"

"I'm fine."

"Would you like to come in?" he offered, with a slight bow.

I hesitated. This behavior was completely at odds with the way he'd acted before. It made me nervous. "Um … no, thanks. I just couldn't stand the thought of us getting off on the wrong foot. I can't deny I sensed you in there, but really, I wasn't trying to spy on you. My curiosity got the better of me. For that, I'm very sorry."

"I hope that is true, Miss Manetas. I do not cherish the thought of you accidentally seeing something private between the guests I occasionally host and me."

I had to force myself not to gape at him. He actually brought people here? In the state that his home was in, I hoped the guests he was talking about were raccoons. "Yeah, about that. I was wondering if you might need a housekeeper. I don't have much to do in my spare time, and your front room could use a woman's touch." Or a blowtorch to get rid of the spiders.

He looked … well, wary. "You want to clean the house?"

"Yes. You have a beautiful home. You really shouldn't leave it in such disrepair."

I expected him to be offended, but he nodded as if he readily agreed. "It does need a little work."

"I could start right now if you'd like."

"That sounds reasonable. How much should I pay you for your services?"

I waved his worries away. "Oh, I don't need any payment. I just need something to occupy my time."

Occupy my time. Ha! It was more like I needed something to keep me from trying to sex up every redneck I heard driving by in their pickup truck.

Mr. Raine's expression was skeptical, but understandably so. He didn't know me, and I didn't know him. Yet, here I was, asking to clean his home. And here he was, willing to let me do it when he was at his most stake-able.

"Won't you come in?" he asked, opening the front door. "The sunrise is upon us. I must seek shelter soon."

"Sure," I said quickly. I didn't want to offend him by showing my fear … again.

I followed him into the house, all while sending up a silent prayer I wouldn't end up with my face on the side of a milk carton. If there was ever a monumentally bad idea, this had to be it. Mr. Raines was not only a total stranger to me, but he was also a vampire. So, basically, that made him a strange vampire, totally the kind of person you should follow into a dingy, filthy house when no one knew your whereabouts.

My fear turned into reality the second he closed the door behind me. Growling low, he pressed my back against the door with his body. His lips hovered near my ear. "Is it sex you're after, Miss Manetas?"

I groaned, unable to hold it inside. The close proximity of his body to mine made keeping it in impossible.

His smile was vicious and all fangs. "Tell me, nymph. Is it my cock you want?"

I pushed against his hard chest to give myself some room. Hell, yes, I wanted his cock. I wanted to drop to my knees on this filthy floor and take him in my mouth until he came, but I would never give him the satisfaction. He was playing a game with me. That callous smile of his gave it away.

"I meant to make amends," I hissed. "And all you mean to do is make fun of me because of my nature. Your pleasure may come from the blood you drink, and mine, from anonymous sex, but I am hardly any different than you. We both need something from someone else. We're both parasites. As far as I can tell, the only difference between us is that I didn't accuse you of wanting my blood when you went all seductive captor on me. I was trying to be civil, something you obviously have no idea how to do."

He released me from the confines of his arms and reopened the door. "Leave, little nymph. I grow bored with you."

I smiled sweetly, though I wanted to punch him in his ridiculously handsome face. "Goodbye, Mr. Raines."

Returning my saccharine smile, he said, "The name is Obsidian, Korrina. And you should know, drinking blood is not the only way I achieve my pleasure."

DEVIL IN A SUNDAY SUIT

KORRINA

October 4th

What is it with supernatural males? A nymph just can't catch a break with them. If they aren't throwing you under the bus for public sex, they were accusing you of wanting to rape them in their own homes. Okay, yes, I would have fucked Obsidian until sundown if he wanted me to, but to accuse me of seeking him out for sex was just hurtful. As was shutting a door in my face. I do have some self-control. Well, most of the time I do.

K

A few hermitical days later, about the time I started wondering if someone could actually die from mundaneness, I had my first real visitor. I sprinted down the hallway at the first peal of the doorbell. I didn't care who it was, as long as it promised some kind of stimulation that didn't involve a broom and dustpan. There was only so many times I could clean a floor that wasn't dirty.

What was revealed behind the door wasn't exactly what I expected. But, honestly, who expects a fiercely sexy man to come calling out of the blue? Cautious, I gave the man a small smile and asked, "Can I help you?"

The stranger returned my smile with interest, exposing slightly sharpened canines in the process. "I sure hope so. Might you be Miss Korrina Manetas?"

Who was this guy? Tax collector? Jehovah's Witness? Local rapist? I tried to gauge his expression, but his blue-green eyes were unreadable.

Warily, I answered, "Yes, I'm Korrina."

He reached into his suit pocket, extracted a letter addressed to me, and handed it over with another winning smile. It was from my mother.

"Thank you, Mr....? I'm sorry I didn't catch your name."

His chuckle was deep and nearly a growl. "That's because I didn't throw it yet. I'm Oswin Morris."

"As in, Oswin Enterprises?"

"Yes, Ma'am."

"Well, come on in, neighbor. Would you like a glass of sweet tea, or can I get you a cup of coffee?"

"Tea would be great."

I stepped back and let the sexy businessman walk into the house. As he passed me, he sniffed the air at the same moment I was able to pick up the wild energy he was throwing off. We glanced at each other's faces, both of us now fully realizing what the other was.

"I-I'll just get that tea," I stammered. "Have a seat in the parlor. It's the first door to your right."

Oswin, ignoring my suggestion, followed me as I hurried back to the kitchen and skidded to a stop in front of the cabinet to get a glass. My hands were trembling like crazy. A werewolf was a perfectly respectable creature for anyone to associate with. A nymph, however, wasn't as acceptable. Our negative reputation always preceded us.

"Here, let me get that," he said, taking the pitcher from my grip. "Sit yourself down, Korrina. You're a wreck."

"I'm sorry. I'm not used to visitors. It's so isolated out here in the country."

He quirked a golden eyebrow in disbelief. "That's not entirely the truth now, is it?"

How well he knew me already. "No. No, it's not. I'm ashamed."

"Of your species? Never be ashamed of that. We are all as

17

God made us. Whether we despise it or not," he added, in a self-depreciating voice.

"That's nice of you to say, Oswin." I wondered if he really meant it.

"Say, hell. I meant every word. We get our fair share of criticism, too."

That was hard to believe. Yes, there was some talk of incest and crazy brother-sister wolves, but the majority considered werewolves the most superior of all the preternatural creatures. "Is that true? Really?"

"Really."

Shyly, I smiled up at him. "Thanks."

He sat across from me, his arms dwarfing the top of the small, two-person bistro table. "I'm always willing to help a beautiful female."

"I'm sure you have a plethora of beautiful females in the pack back home to help. What brings you here?"

"The mailman around these parts is getting on in years, and lately, he's had trouble reading the numbers. I wanted to make sure you got your mail."

He stroked my cheek, and I all but melted into the huge hand cupping my face. Stupid nymph hormones.

"I might have been a little intrigued by the new arrival at the old Raines place, too," he admitted.

I groaned inwardly, thinking about the Raines descendent living next door. Coincidence? Yeah, right. "Raines?" I ventured.

"Yeah. The Raines family built this place back in the early eighteen-hundreds. There's another house almost identical about a half mile up the road. To be honest, I tried to buy both of the houses once, but the owner was reluctant to sell. I'm kind of glad he didn't sell to me now that I've met you."

"You're quite the smooth talker aren't you?"

"I reckon. How am I doing so far with you, lovely one?"

I sighed, feigning nonchalance. "I've heard better lines."

"Well, then give me a chance to do better. Go out with me tomorrow night."

Quickly tamping down the inner nymph that was jumping for joy, I asked, "Don't you live in Thomasville? That's a pretty long drive to come and pick me up."

Leaning forward, he gently kissed me on the lips. "I think it'll be worth it."

After that kiss, I couldn't disagree. Oswin was a delightful and welcome surprise. Not ten minutes after his arrival, he was able to leave me with the only genuine smile I'd had in weeks. And for the first time in my life, that was way more important to me than the prowess he might have in the bedroom.

***

A few hours after America's sexiest werewolf left, I finally came down from my new love interest high and remembered he'd brought me a letter, which reminded me I hadn't checked to see if I'd gotten any others. Smiling to myself, I walked to the porch, lifted the flap on the old-fashioned mailbox, and was pleasantly surprised by what I found. There was only one item, but it was an impressive thick parchment envelope, obviously an invitation. Only, it didn't have a return address, just my name in calligraphy across the front.

Excited about my first letters since I moved in, I rushed back inside and sat down to open my mother's letter first, savoring the invitation's excitement. Just as I imagined it would be, her letter was chock full of news of more babies. That was no surprise. With all my brothers and sisters, I had many nieces and nephews already.

Assured that life was going on without me in Meadowbrook, I quickly scanned the rest and set her letter aside to open the invitation. I was glad I did. The invitation was for dinner at

Obsidian's house at nine o'clock. I looked at the clock—seven fifty-seven. I didn't have much time to get ready. Would he be upset if I didn't show at all? I debated that for a few more nanoseconds before running like a madwoman to my room to get dressed. If he was willing to be civil, so was I.

I stood in front of the closet in a panic. Flicking through the hangers, I worried Obsidian would disapprove of my clothing choice. Besides jeans and t-shirts, most of my wardrobe was tight, short, and revealing. I had no idea what the dress code was for a vampire dinner, but I was pretty sure he wouldn't appreciate me wearing my favorite little black dress. He had been in a crisp suit every time I'd seen him. No doubt, he would expect me to dress in a similar fashion.

Two minutes of frantic searching later, I settled on a deep blue strapless dress with a full skirt. I'd worn it to my high school's ten-year reunion. It was sexy, but classy enough for the most formal occasion. Along with the dress, I grabbed the diamond studs from my jewelry box, my sparkly blue shoes, and my makeup bag on the way to the bathroom. Once there, I agonized over how to style my hair. Should I wear it up to accentuate my long neck, or was that a terrible idea, given his undead status? Ultimately, I chose to pin my long dark curls up, leaving a few wisps down to frame my face. A dab of perfume and a blood red painted mouth completed the look. With a sigh at my reflection, I pronounced myself ready and walked out the door. It was the best I could do on such short notice.

***

At eight fifty-five, I pulled into Obsidian's driveway. A little apprehensive, I sat in near hyperventilation as I stared at his house. I wasn't sure what I was doing here. He'd been nothing short of awful to me every time we'd been together. It was almost as if accepting his invitation was a mistake I just couldn't help making.

At one minute before the hour, Obsidian came out to the porch to see what was taking me so long. I shivered when I saw him. He was so unbelievably handsome as he stood there staring back at me. Even with the possibility of something happening with Oswin, I couldn't help but hope he had something romantic planned for tonight. Surely, this wasn't just for my forgiveness.

"Are you going to get out of the car?" he asked, chuckling a bit as he walked down the front steps.

"I'm kind of waiting for the other shoe to drop," I called out the window.

He leaned on the hood of my car with an amused smile on his lips "I can assure you that nothing untoward will occur tonight. You are safe here."

I arched a disbelieving eyebrow. Uh huh. Wasn't that what all serial killers told their victims before they cut them up into tiny little pieces?

"I promise, Korrina," he pressed. "You have my word."

Out of all logical reasons to stall, I took a deep breath and opened the door, grimacing when my dress caught on something under the seat. "Really?" I griped, wobbling on my high heels as I tried fruitlessly to dislodge the fabric.

Obsidian sped to my side. "Are you okay?"

I laughed nervously and shrugged. "I don't know. Has anyone ever died from embarrassment?"

The corners of Obsidian's eyes crinkled as he barked out a loud, genuine laugh. "Not that I'm aware of." He crouched down to inspect the underside of the seat. "May I help you?"

"Sure," I said, my voice shaking with emotion. There was something about this vampire. When he was close to me, my body responded in a way it never had. I was a nymph, true. But Obsidian Raines made me want to be careless. And I knew, when it came down to it, I would do anything to have him.

As if he could hear my thoughts, Obsidian never took his eyes away from mine as he deftly loosened the dress from whatever was holding it hostage and straightened. Once upright, he gave me a knowing smile and offered his arm to me. "Shall we?"

I nodded, momentarily mute with hunger. I had a strong feeling, if everything went well, I would end up with my panties around my ankles after dinner. I really, really, really wanted that to happen.

Eager to fill the silence between us, I said, "Thank you for the invitation, Obsidian. And for helping me with my dress."

"It is my pleasure. You are a vision tonight. It would have been a shame to see your dress ruined."

I stared at the ground as a hot blush crept across my face. "Thank you."

"You're welcome," he murmured softly. "I'm pleased you joined me tonight. I was unsure of whether you would come after our last ... battle of wills."

"That's a nice way of saying 'fight', right?"

He opened the front door and smiled down at me with guileless amber eyes. "By no means."

I laughed at his attempt to downplay our mutual anger and followed him into the house. Once inside, my face morphed into stunned delight. "It's beautiful, Obsidian."

And it was. Everything, from floor to ceiling, was sparkling clean and polished. Gone was the sheet-covered furniture, dusty floorboards, and grimy crystal chandeliers that looked so terrible only a few days ago. Now they shined brightly in the glow of a candlelit table set for two. To complete the ambiance of the room and leave no doubt that this was meant to be a date, a vase of blood-red roses adorned every window.

He patted my hand. "Accept my apologies for not telling you about the maid service. I promise I haven't forgotten about the arrangement you asked for." He lifted my hand to his mouth and pressed his lips to my knuckles. "I just wanted everything to be perfect for you.

I stepped forward and stood on the tips of my toes to brush a soft kiss on his cheek. "Thank you."

Obsidian caught my arms as I pulled away, then he leaned toward me to scent the air. "Korrina, why do you smell of wolf?"

"I had a visitor today," I answered, surprised that he could discern Oswin's scent over my perfume. "Ironically, he was also returning a letter that was delivered to the wrong address. He said the mailman is really old."

"The mailman is twenty-four," he said quickly. "Who was your visitor?"

"It was our neighbor, Oswin Morris."

"Was that all Mr. Morris wanted?" he asked, looking agitated.

"Yeah, why? What's wrong? Do you know him?"

"Far too well, I'm afraid." He loosened his grip on my arms and grimly pulled out a chair for me, waiting for me to sit before he took the chair across the table. "Look, I know Oswin seems like an honorable male; he puts on a great show. He's an Alpha, Korrina. Putting on a show of strength and dominance is a part of life for them. But trust me on this. Oswin is not a nice male. Not even close. And if he's sniffing around your place, you can be sure he wants something from you. Make no mistake about that."

I shrugged and tried not to look sheepish. "He wants to date me is all. He asked me out for tomorrow night."

"No."

I froze, staring at him like I'd never seen him before. Had my ears deceived me, or did he really just tell me that I couldn't do something?

"What do you mean, no?" I asked experimentally. I thought it best to test the waters before I handed him his ass on a platter because he kind of looked like he was going to have an aneurysm.

"I will not permit you to go on this 'date'."

With perfect poise, I calmly crossed my legs and said, "I don't need your permission, Obsidian. I'm not yours to command."

"On this, you will obey me!" he demanded angrily, his eyes pure black.

"Okay, I think we're done here," I told him, standing up.

Rushing to his feet, he grazed a hand down my arm. "I only ask this for your safety."

"I don't remember you asking me anything," I countered, snatching my arm away from him. "I remember you insisting that I obey you. But see, there's one thing you don't know about me. I don't take orders from you or anyone else."

An uncustomary kindness filled his amber eyes as he said, "Korrina, I have thought of little else but you these past few nights. I like you, and I need you to be safe. I cannot bear the thought of you with someone so corrupt and conniving, especially during the day when I cannot help you. I'm not kidding around when I say he's dangerous."

I shook my head. Did I just step into the Twilight Zone? Wasn't he the same insensitive vampire that accused me of trying to seduce him the other day? Now he liked me, wanted me to be safe, and was making romantic overtures? What the hell was going on with this guy?

"Are you well?" I asked. "I mean, did you drink bad blood or something?"

My sudden change of topic made his brows furrow. "I'm fine. Why would you ask such a thing?"

"Honestly, because I think you're either bipolar, or you have no idea how to court a female."

"How would you know?" he shot back. "How many times in your life have you been courted?"

Okay, that one stung a little.

"Don't be ridiculous," I told him. "I've had many lovers."

He scoffed. "Of that, I've no doubt."

Right there. That was the moment I completely lost my shit. Rearing back, I slapped Obsidian's face so hard he fell to the floor. He was back on his feet and spitting mad half a second later, but I couldn't care less. His twisted little game had just lost a player. "Don't call on me," I hissed through gritted teeth. "Ever."

Without another word, I slammed the door behind me and stormed to my car. That self-righteous, pompous asshole! I just couldn't believe I went to all the trouble of getting dressed up, only to have him treat me like a slut. Well, he wouldn't have the chance to do it again. This was it, the nail in the fucking coffin. Obsidian Raines was dead to me. No puns intended.

***

After the short trip back to my house, I stomped my way up the stairs and made a beeline to where I'd stuck Oswin's business card. Damn it, scared or not, I would make Obsidian pay for what he'd done tonight. I would make sure he was every bit as livid as he'd made me. And I couldn't think of a better way to do that than invite someone he hated into my bed for some very loud, very enthusiastic werewolf sex.

Grabbing my cell from the nightstand, I hastily punched in his number then held my breath as I listened to it ring.

"Hello?" Oswin asked.

"Hey, Oswin. I'm sorry for calling you so late."

"Is this my little nymph?"

"Your nymph?" I purred back.

His chuckle turned into a low, growling vocalization. "That's right. Did you need something, darlin'?"

"I'm fine," I said, smiling to myself. It was nice to have someone who cared enough to ask. "I just wanted to say that I can't wait to see you tomorrow."

"Me, either, sugar. I've been thinking of you the whole drive back. What time is it getting to be?"

I leaned back to look at my alarm clock. "Five after nine."

"So, that gives me two hours and fifty-five minutes until tomorrow, right?"

My grin widened. "That's right."

"Good. See you tomorrow, Korrina."

"Tomorrow, Oswin."

I clicked off the phone and ran to the bathroom. The Oswin situation had just gone to DEFCON Level 3. Sex was imminent. Obsidian wasn't going to know what hit him.

HOWLING WITH A WOLF

KORRINA

October 4th

Obsidian Raines ... what a freakin' asshole! Seriously, the man needs medication. A lot of it. I'm not going to dwell on it, though. Tonight, I'm going to remedy the bad taste he's put in my mouth by fucking Oswin until I can't see straight. I. Can't. Wait.

K

At eleven fifty-eight, the doorbell rang. Excited, I let out a giddy squeal and ran down the stairs two at a time to fling the door open. I was more than ready to wrap myself around Oswin's hard body.

I just wish my senses had registered that my visitor wasn't Oswin a few seconds earlier. My arms flailed out uselessly as I tried to stop my forward momentum. I ended up falling right into Obsidian's waiting grasp.

"I take it you accept my apology?" he asked, laughing as he ran his fingers down the silky material at my sides.

I grabbed his hands and pushed them back at him. "I most certainly do not. I thought you were someone else."

Obsidian was nonplussed. "A midnight rendezvous—you naughty female. Who is the lucky fellow?"

"That would be me," a deep voice growled. "Are you all right, Korrina?"

Oswin stood stock still in the porch light, his murderous expression making him look wild and more than ready to take the male on. Obsidian's face looked much the same, but his anger seemed to be directed at me. Recoiling, I backed away from him.

He shook his head at me in disgust. "I should have guessed

you'd fuck the first dick that—"

With a roar, Oswin lunged forward, tackling him. A second later, they both went tumbling off the porch. The railing didn't even come close to slowing them down. It was terrible of me, but as I watched them throw punch after punch at each other in awe, I hoped Oswin had the presence of mind to stake him with some of the wreckage. I was getting really tired of the constant barrage of insults. Obsidian barely knew me, and yet, he was content to degrade me at every turn. I could only take so much before I snapped.

And, apparently, neither could Obsidian. Using his vampire speed for momentum, I watched him shove Oswin so hard, his body made a crater in the ground when he landed. It would only give him a second to escape, but that was all he needed. He raced in the direction of his house faster than I could follow with my eyes.

Oswin appeared right after him, his eyes wolf yellow. "What the hell was that about, Korrina? What's he doing here?"

I leaned against the doorframe and sighed. "I think to apologize."

He frowned and yanked off what was left of the porch's handrail. "You need security cameras and stronger doors. Obsidian Raines isn't known around here for his winning personality. He's known as a killer. Why do you think he's chosen to live in such an isolated area?"

I stared at Oswin. Was he serious? Obsidian was the quintessential scary vampire and a gigantic dick, but he didn't seem unbalanced enough for murder. And there had been no deaths or disappearances since I'd moved in. I wondered what he knew that I didn't. "I'll call someone in the morning," I told him. "I can't believe my neighbor is a murderer."

"Vampires don't usually come right out and tell you, you know."

"No, I guess not. He did, however, tell me that you aren't an

28

honorable male."

His brows raised in surprise. "Did he? I won't lie. I've done a few things I'm not proud of."

"Like lie about the age of the mailman?" I asked, hands on hips.

Chagrined, he smiled again, this time throwing a little charm into it. "All right, you got me. I may have paid the mailman to mistake your address for mine accidentally. I saw you taking out the trash while I was out here the other day. I wanted a reason to meet you."

"Well, I'm glad you did. And I'm glad you drove back out here. I was hoping you would come."

He gave me a grin that was all wolf. "With you here, how could I not come?"

I couldn't tell if his words were a double entendre or not. I couldn't care less. Grabbing his hand, I pulled him inside, shut the door, and seized his lapels to pull him down to my mouth in a desperate kiss.

He was hard and wild as he quickly took control. "Bedroom?" he asked, sliding his hands down my hips and cupping my ass to lift me up.

I wrapped my legs around his waist and groaned from the delicious friction. "Up the stairs, first door on the left. Hurry."

Oswin ran up the stairs, taking the steps three at a time. He was a lot stronger than I'd thought and a lot faster, and, holy shit, he was rock hard. Kissing me roughly, he brought blood to my lip before lowering me to my feet. "Korrina, I'm trying really hard to be a gentle-male here."

I pulled the red negligée I wore over my head and dropped it to the floor, revealing my nakedness. "There's really no need for restraint."

For a split-second, Oswin seemed stunned by what I'd

uncovered. The shock didn't last for long. He stalked toward me, fangs fully extended. His eyes had lost every bit of the humanity I'd seen there before. "Run," he whispered. "So I can catch you."

Without a moment's hesitation, I bolted, pushing myself to move faster than I ever had before. But even with my supernatural speed, I only made it a few steps out of the bedroom before he caught me around the middle. He took me down to the floor like prey, gripping my shoulder in between his sharpened teeth and growling a loud commandeering snarl. This wasn't a request. He would have me now.

In response, I arched my back and ground against his erection, boldly offering myself to him. "Oswin, please," I begged him, wanting more. "Please."

Groaning, he slipped his arm around my ribcage, pulling me vertical against his chest and holding me there by my throat. "You drive my wolf crazy, Korrina," he said through gnashed teeth, panting heavily into my hair. "You'll have to pardon me if this only lasts a minute."

I screamed as he plunged into me all at once, unable to hold it in. He was so damn … big. He stilled, sensing my distress and gave me a moment to adjust to his size.

"You okay?" he asked, nuzzling the side of my neck as if to ask for forgiveness.

I laughed shakily. "I think so."

"I'm sorry. I just assumed with you being a nymph…"

"Don't you dare finish that sentence," I interrupted.

"You are different from any other female I've known," he said, chuckling into my hair.

Encircling his thighs with my calves, I asked, "How so?"

He groaned as I spread myself open for him and cupped my breast with his free hand. "You're brave," he told me, growling softly. "But I wonder. Are you brave enough to take what I want to give you right now?"

"Yes," I moaned, glad to take whatever he was willing to give. It had been far too long since I'd had an orgasm that wasn't produced manually.

"Good." He rolled my nipple between his fingers and started to move inside me. At first, he was gentle, testing in his movements. But soon, he was thrusting into me with speed only a supernatural being was capable of.

Gasping, I held on to the strong arm across my chest, trying hard to keep up with the brutal rhythm he'd set. Within seconds, I screamed out in orgasm. Oswin's own climax was quick to follow. He spilled into me with a roar that shook plaster off the ceiling. I held on to him limply, praying he'd give me a few minutes to heal before wanting me again. Sex with a werewolf wasn't something I was used to.

But it was definitely something I wanted to get used to.

When our heartbeats finally started to slow, he lowered me to my knees and pulled out, though he was still fully erect. I turned to face him. His smile was devilish, his eyes as yellow as citrine. There was no doubt his wolf was close to the surface.

"Oh, I'm not done with you, darlin'," he said. "Not by a long shot. But before I take you again—and I will be taking you again tonight, I think I should get out of this suit."

"Well then, let's get you naked." I loosened his tie with one hand while rhythmically stroking his still slick erection with the other. He groaned loudly and bucked into my hand. "Weren't you going to get out of your clothes, Mr. Morris?" I teased.

"Yes," he growled, and in seconds, he was gloriously bare-chested, his expensive suit in shreds around us.

Wow. Werewolves were hardcore.

Intrigued, I used both hands to wrap around his girth, pumping slowly, working him closer to another orgasm. I knew how hard it must be for him to let me heal when he was still so hard, so ready for me. I wasn't about to disappoint him. Arching my back, I lowered my mouth to his length, making sure that I lifted my backside for him to get his fill (or feel) of. Werewolves were a sucker for a nice ass—naturally, and he was no different.

I ran my tongue up the underside of him from base to tip, smiling smugly when his breath hitched. He returned my smile with a cunning one of his own and tangled his hands in my hair. Holding my head still, he pumped himself into my welcoming mouth. Apparently, he was a male that was used to being in complete control—in every way. Breathing hard, he barked out my name only seconds later, taking his massive cock in hand and emptying his seed onto my breasts.

"Fuck, Korrina," he panted. "Point me in the general direction of the shower."

I chuckled. "I'll show you if I can walk."

"No need, darlin'," he assured me, swinging me up into his arms. He paused to kick his pants free of his feet and carried me in the direction I indicated, his dick still hard as a rock.

Oh boy. What did I get myself into?

THINGS JUST GOT INTERESTING

OSWIN

I sped toward Thomasville with a feeling I hadn't felt in a very long time. From the moment our eyes met, I knew. I knew Korrina would be the answer to ... everything. Finding someone like her, at the time I needed her the most, was a dream. It was almost too serendipitous to believe it was real.

Even more unexpected was her letting me into her bed ... well, floor and shower, so quickly. Nymph or not, I knew how scared she must have been to lie with me. I was Oswin Morris, the big bad Alpha wolf known by a nasty reputation that was one-hundred-percent true. She should have been terrified.

But, to my surprise, there had been no fear. Last night, Korrina had presented me with a flawless combination of calm, skill, and uninhibited hunger that was far beyond her age. The latter, more than any. Perfect wasn't a word I threw around often, but, man, as I took a last look at her naked body on my way out this morning, she was the closest thing to perfection I'd ever seen.

And if all that wasn't fantastic enough, she liked me. There was no doubt about that. I had been worried when I saw the vampire at her door, but after the intense night we'd spent together, my fears were gone. She would be mine. And she couldn't have come at a better time. With the pack being so unsettled, I needed to take a mate both for stability and to keep my seat as Alpha. I had been without one too long. It wasn't something I could put off forever. Korrina would make all that bearable. She was immortal, gorgeous, keen on fucking me, and more importantly, just a really nice female.

***

Thoughts of my green-eyed, raven-haired temptress, peppered in with thoughts of my deceitful pack, kept me occupied for most

33

of the drive back to Thomasville. I despised the idea of bringing my sweet-natured bride-to-be into the midst of so much chaos, but it had to be done. What was left of the good wolves in the pack needed her. They needed peace.

I pulled onto the red dirt road that led to what my parents had fashioned into a makeshift pack-lands. There were a few houses built on the lands. Most of the wolves lived in old trailers I'd picked up at auctions. My father had employed the "keep the lower wolves lower, and they'll have no choice but to respect you" tactic, making them sleep in tents and ramshackle shacks while he was Alpha. I would not do that. I had no interest in keeping the pack down. I wanted them to flourish.

And that had worked well, for a time. Not anymore. Today, martial law reigned supreme. Guards were watching over me and my home twenty-four seven. When they weren't running off the steady stream of females that wanted to throw their hat in the ring for Alpha female, that is. The wolves were salivating over the vacancy, and they didn't mind sacrificing their daughters to me, no matter how well-deserved my reputation was.

Arriving at my modest home, I nodded to my two personal guards as I unlocked the front door and asked about their wives, hoping they wouldn't notice my suit had been replaced with the old work clothes I kept in my truck. No such luck.

"Someone got lucky last night," Scott said, a wide grin spread across his face. "You owe me a twenty, Pete."

Pete rolled his alert yellow eyes and fished the twenty out of his pocket. "Is that nymph I detect, Mr. Morris?"

I sighed. Damn their werewolf senses. "Yes, but keep it to yourself. I don't want the females getting stirred up. They're already driving me crazy."

"Yeah, about that." Scott reached into his satchel and handed me a manila envelope. "Bailey dropped this off for you."

"What's in here?" I asked warily.

He grinned again and waggled his blond eyebrows. "Naked pictures."

I peeked inside the envelope and shuddered. "They are relentless."

"That, they are," Pete agreed. He shook his dark head. "I've never seen anything like it."

"Hopefully, you won't see it for much longer. I think things are headed in the right direction with my new lady."

Scott let out a low whistle. "They won't thank you for bringing in an outsider, especially one from a completely different species."

"They won't thank me for anything," I told him. "So that's pretty much a moot point."

Scott clapped me on the back on my way through the door. "One day at a time, eh, boss?"

"One day at a time," I echoed.

Once inside, I let out a breath and thanked the Lord a she-wolf didn't get a whiff of me on the way in. I'd never hear the end of it if they found out I'd been with Korrina. I looked at the envelope full of naked werewolf in my hand, shuddered again, and found the nearest garbage can. Korrina could not have come too soon.

I stripped down and was just about to step into the shower when the doorbell rang. Irritated, I wrapped a towel around my hips and padded to the front door, sighing heavily when I saw my least favorite person on the other side of the glass. Tall and blonde, Patricia mirrored most of the wolves. There was so much inbreeding in my father's pack, I was sure half of them were related to me somehow.

"What can I do for you, Patricia?" I asked, stepping onto the porch.

Before she answered, she inhaled deeply and growled. "What the fuck, Oswin? You've got the whole pack to choose from, and you go fuck some whore nymph?"

"She's not a whore, and I don't appreciate the tone," I growled back.

"If you're looking for someone to suck your cock, Oswin, I'll do it. Make me the Alpha, and I'll do it morning, noon, and night. I'll let you do whatever you want to me. That's the kind of thing you get off on, right?"

"Patricia, it's none of your concern what gets me off. You could never be my mate. I need a female that wants me as a person, as a lover. No one in the pack can give me that, including you."

Her alluring smile turned to a smirk full of hate. "You're a fucking embarrassment to our race," she spat. "You think we don't know about the things you've done? We know about the sick, depraved things you've done to get what you want. You think you're so much better than us because you have money. You don't know shit."

Stung by her words, I took a step forward. "If you don't like the things your Alpha does, if I'm so fucking terrible, feel free to leave the pack."

She glared at me before storming off the porch. "It's not me that should leave."

FRIENDS ARE FOR SUCKERS

OBSIDIAN

Last night had been interesting … and eye-opening. I had so much faith in my strength and power, it never occurred to me that someone might get the drop on me. Oswin taught me just how wrong I was about that. Though the bleeding had almost stopped by the time I finally made it back to the house, I spent a good portion of the night doubled over from the sharp stings of pain in my sides. I could only grit my teeth and wait for my broken ribs to mend themselves. It was never a pleasant experience and was exactly the kind of injury that was a prime example of why I had stayed out of sight. There is no hope of drama when you live as a recluse. And no fucking werewolves.

With my broken ribs a not so distant memory, I went about my life as usual. I cleaned the bathtub. I made the bed. But I just couldn't forget what I'd heard last night. Listening to Korrina and Oswin Morris have sex was probably both the most annoying and heartbreaking sound in the world. I had pitied her when I heard her plaintive screams and whimpers. No doubt, he wasn't gentle. Not like it should have been. Not like I would have been with her.

By the next afternoon, I had worked myself into a fine froth over the entire situation. I was pissed and fucking sick to death of Oswin's Alpha syndrome. Werewolves were so tiresome, continually obsessing over being the biggest, baddest creature in town. And Morris was no different than the wolves I met before him—always looking to dick around with vampires. Never mind that we could easily break into their pitiful camp and suck them dry before the first howl of alarm sounded in their sensitive ears. Their strength and agility could never compare to ours, though they loved to test the theory whenever they saw an opportunity.

Well, if a morally bankrupt werewolf was the kind of male Korrina wanted in her bed, so be it. The wolf could have her. As much as I craved her, I didn't need the distraction. Besides, she'd caused enough aggravation for me to last a lifetime, even one as long as mine.

***

Presumably, to drive me crazy, Korrina came by the house as soon as the sun went down. I was sure it was her, even before I caught her scent, by the stern little rap against the glass of the door. And while it irritated me that she'd come here after what I had to endure, I knew I couldn't not answer the door. As stubborn as the nymph was, she'd probably keep coming back until I did. Besides, with her senses, she'd know I was here.

Sighing with what felt like the weight of the world on my shoulders, I strode to the door and jerked it open. "Whatever you are peddling, I'm not buying," I said, though what I really wanted was to tell her how much I wanted to be the one that made her scream with orgasm.

Korrina's expression flashed from calm, to shocked, then back to angry before she growled, "I'm not peddling anything, you fucking asshole. I just came over to make sure you didn't die from your injuries ... and to apologize. I'm sorry Oswin hurt you last night. That wasn't what I wanted."

"Wasn't it?" I asked doubtfully.

She pursed her lips. "Okay, maybe for a split second, I might have thought that you deserved what you got for saying the things you did. You were completely out of line. And you hurt my feelings."

Her face blushed a delicate pink, and I immediately felt an all-consuming urge to invite her in. She smelled so good, so sweet and fragrant, I had to clench my hands to keep from grabbing her and pressing her slender neck to my mouth. I was startled by the aching need. I'd never wanted something so much it made my mouth water before. I'd always prided myself on having a strong moral fiber, unlike so many made vampires. But with Korrina, I couldn't seem to control myself.

Fumbling for the words that would convince her to leave, I finally said, "Korrina, if I offended your..." I arched a disbelieving brow, knowing it would add to the insult. "Delicate sensibilities, I apologize."

Stomping her tiny foot, she let out a frustrated scream. "Why do you always do that? You know damn well you offended me! I tend to get a little provoked when I'm consistently called a slut. I'm not, you know."

"Maybe not, but have you ever had sex for love, Korrina?"

Her flush deepened. "Uh ... what?"

I leaned against the doorframe. "Have you ever taken a male between your legs because you loved him?"

"I really don't see how that's any of your business."

I smirked. "I'll take that as a 'no', then?"

She pushed her unruly dark hair away from her face in irritation. "No, all right? I've never made love, but that's not really that shocking since I've never been in love."

I stepped closer. "A hazard of being what you are, I guess?"

Weary of our bickering, she sighed. "Obsidian, you don't give being an individual very much credit, do you? Regardless of what you might think about me, I still plan on marrying and having young. I'm not going to end up like some of the other nymphs. No one in my family ever has."

"Time will tell," I said, shrugging with indifference.

"Nope," she said. "I'm not going to let you piss me off again. That shit is over." She pointed to a bucket on the top step. "I brought my cleaning stuff today. Where do you want me to begin?"

Fear struck me in the pit of my stomach. She couldn't stay. There was no way I would be able to resist the delicate curve of her neck. The injuries I suffered last night had taken nearly all of my strength. I needed to feed, now.

"I'm sorry," I said, shaking my head. "You can't start today."

The tiniest of furrows appeared between her brows. "Why? Give me one good reason that doesn't involve your disapproval of my sex life."

I scrubbed a hand over my face. Was I really going to tell her this? Yes. Yes, I was. "Korrina, I have to feed."

"What? Now?" she asked, her eyes wide with alarm.

I smiled somberly, not at all offended by her fear. "I don't intend on feeding on you. I promise."

"On who, then? You won't kill them, will you?"

"Of course not," I assured her. "You've already met most of my blood sources."

"I have? Who are they?"

I paced the porch, avoiding her gaze. "The townspeople, the mailman, the grocery store clerks, the pastor … you know, the town."

Her mouth dropped open. "All of them? So, who is the main course tonight?"

She had asked an excellent question. Who was going to provide me with a meal tonight? I'd already hypnotized every soul in town to prevent them from remembering me, some of them more than once. I needed to expand my search for victims.

When I didn't answer right away, she frowned and looked curiously at my face. "You still here with me?"

"I am. I just don't have an answer to your question."

She pursed her lips. "You are biting the willing, aren't you?"

"Yes, I only feed from the willing." It wasn't a lie. The townspeople were always quite willing after they'd been hypnotized.

No human really believes in vampires. They think I'm just a handsome man with a kinky fetish and a good orthodontist. None of the ones who were brave enough to submit to me willingly had ever returned for a second feeding. Perhaps they had expected more in return. If they had, they were giving our kind more credit than we deserved. Desire and thirst were the only emotions we were usually capable of. The wants of others were inconsequential. Even I couldn't deny being that callous most of the time.

"How do you sign up to be a donor?"

I stared down at her, unsure of what her question implied. Was she just curious or was she offering herself up? "I've advertised," I lied. "They come to me."

She seemed relieved. "Good. Do they like to be bitten? I mean, what's in it for them?"

I grinned, fangs completely emerged. She wanted me to feed from her. I could smell the heavenly scent of her desire. "That is a conversation that requires privacy. Will you come in?"

Warily, she obliged. I closed the door behind her, my supernatural vision detecting a tremble in her hand, though it was evident that she was trying to hide it from me. "You're jumpy, Korrina. Is it the subject matter?"

"Maybe," she admitted.

"Are you afraid I will attack you, or are you afraid you will offer yourself to me?"

Bright green eyes met mine. "Both."

Her answer made my teeth ache. "I can show you how it feels if you'd like. The experience is difficult to describe."

She bit her lip. "Does it hurt?"

I grinned again. "Only if you want it to."

She stared at my eager smile for a moment then closed the distance between us. Pulling her hair to the side, she slipped an arm around my neck and murmured, "Consider this a peace offering between us, Obsidian."

If anyone had cared to make peace before, I couldn't remember it. It was as if she actually cared to ally herself with me. I palmed her head and breathed her in. She smelled of vanilla and fragrant spices. Her blood would be sweet, like muscadine wine. "Are you certain you want this, Korrina?"

She hesitated only a moment. "If it gains me your friendship, then yes, I want it."

The guilt her selflessness brought on was unexpected. She wanted to be my confidant, and I had only thought of her as a parasite in search of pleasure. Shit. I really was an asshole.

Stepping away, I said, "I'm sorry. I can't do this."

Inexplicable tears sprang to her eyes. "Do you think my blood unsuitable?"

"What? No. Of course not. In fact, I think quite the opposite. You tried to make peace with me even after all the hateful things I've said and done, and all I've done is mock and belittle your attempts. Feeding on you would just be another means of degrading you for my benefit. I am not an evil person. I cannot, in good conscience, take from you when I do not deserve it."

She straightened her neck and smiled. "That was almost an apology."

"You noticed."

"I did, and I have a trade to offer," she suggested. There was a spark of mischief in her eyes.

"If you are about to offer me your blood in exchange to clean my toilet, I hope you have prepared yourself for unhappiness."

She burst into helpless giggles. "No. That wasn't quite what I had in mind."

A weight sank into my chest. I knew what she had in mind. It was what all nymphs wanted, without fail—sex. I sighed. "What is the arrangement you desire?"

"I suggest that in exchange for me feeding you once a week, you agree to keep an ear out for me at my place … and maybe come over for supper and a movie occasionally. Or maybe, we can watch movies, and I can be dinner—whatever works with your schedule."

I stood there unblinking for a few beats of her heart. "You want to be friends?"

"Yes! I'm dying of boredom over there. Last night was the most exciting night I've had since I've moved in."

"Indeed," I countered, revolted at her admission.

She rolled her eyes. "Not the sex, Obsidian. I meant because something actually happened. You have no idea what it's like to be alone all the time."

How wrong she was about that. I knew all too well what crippling loneliness felt like. "That is a sentiment I have a deep understanding of, Korrina. I would be happy to be a friend to you."

Her happy face showed the depth of her appreciation. "Great! So, are you ready to drink?"

I frowned. "I am, but not here."

She looked around. "Where?"

"Follow me." I led her to my bedroom. I wanted her to be comfortable during her first feeding. It would make it easier for her to keep her bargain.

She looked around in amazement when we arrived. "Your home is beautiful. Why did you leave the front room so dirty before?"

"I find that if it appears ominous, it usually keeps the children of the town full of frightening stories and rumors. That discourages them from intruding while I rest."

She laughed. "That was a good idea. It definitely had me spooked."

"About that evening … may I ask you a question?"

She nodded.

"I was sure that you would go home after you'd said your goodbye to the trees. Why did you come here?"

She looked at the floor as if she was embarrassed. "The gardeners were still at the house working. I could hear the lawnmowers."

"You are unlike any nymph I've known." A nymph who didn't want to have sex? Any other of her kind would have done just about anything for the opportunity.

"How many of us have you known?"

"A dozen or so."

"I see we didn't make a great impression, did we?"

I just shook my head. She didn't need to know specifics. Not yet. "You can lie on the bed, and I will take your neck, or if you prefer, I can take your wrist or thigh instead." I hoped like hell she didn't say her thigh.

Korrina walked to the bed and slipped off her heels. Lying back on the pillows, she smoothed out her skirt, making sure she was covered then pulled the long, dark waves of hair away from her neck. "Okay, I'm ready."

I slipped off my shoes and climbed over her onto my knees, unsure if I could go through with this.

Seeing my hesitation, she gave me a reassuring smile. "I'm not afraid."

We'd see about that when the feeding was over. When you've had as many go awry as I've had, you become dubious of new donors. Pushing that fear out of my mind, I hastily lifted her neck toward my mouth, intending to drink until I was sated and then send her on her way.

That was not to be. The moment the scent of her arousal filled my nostrils, my cock began to harden, pressing painfully against my zipper. "I'm sorry! I—" I sputtered, horrified by the reaction.

Why was this be happening now? I hadn't had an erection in over eight years.

She glanced down at the mortifying bulge in my pants. "Obsidian, if you want to make the feeding sexual, I'm open to it. I want you, too. There's no pressure though if you … um … aren't into females."

WANTING MORE THAN I CAN HANDLE
OBSIDIAN

Did I want to make the feeding sexual? Without a doubt. Could I make it sexual? Doubtful. It had been so long since I'd been with anyone, I wasn't sure I could go through with it without some serious thought. She was a nymph. Would she understand that I'd never been anything but monogamous to my late wife? Or would she think me pathetic?

I lowered her head back to the pillow and moved to lie beside her. How was I supposed to say this? Just blurt out my tragedy and hope for the best? Yeah, that sounded good, if not as potentially traumatizing as the rest of the past twenty-four hours had been.

"Korrina," I said, hesitating a few seconds before I spat out my heartache. "I'm a widower."

"I'm so sorry," she replied sympathetically, tears springing to her eyes.

I nodded solemnly. "Thank you. I appreciate it. It's been almost five years since she passed, but I still miss her terribly."

She rolled over to face me and laced the fingers of her right hand with my left. "Tell me about her. Where did you meet?"

I smiled at the memory of meeting my wife. "In the summer of nineteen fifty-five, I moved to New York, where it was rumored to have a higher concentration of potential donors. I met Edith the very night I arrived. She worked as a waitress at a cocktail bar and wasn't especially handsome, but she had a special kind of charisma—a spark—and a very rare AB- blood type. After her shift, I followed her into the alley she used as a shortcut home and attacked her. I was so hungry and certainly wasn't the gentleman I could have been, which she pointed out as she was kneeing me in the goods. She taught me a damn valuable lesson about modern women of the fifties that night. I'll tell you that."

46

Korrina squeezed my hand and grinned. "Edith sounds like my kind of girl."

I nodded. "You would've liked her. Your stubborn streak reminds me a lot of hers. And just like you, she didn't approve of my liberal tongue. She would have kicked my ass for speaking to you the way I did before."

Her eyes twinkled with humor. "Then she was definitely my kind of girl. So, after she forgave you for snacking on her like a walking roast beef sandwich, how long did you see each other before you got married?

"Only a week. It was a poor decision from the start. We were happy for such a short time. We were blind to it at first, but we soon realized how mismatched we were. We were from different worlds."

"But you could have changed her to a vampire, right? If you were so different, why didn't she just become like you."

I sighed. Edith's distaste for my species wasn't something I liked to reminisce about. "I tried to convince her. I begged her over and over. She always rejected it as a reprehensible, cowardly way out of our problems. Eventually, I gave up."

Korrina flinched. "Ouch. That must have been hard, knowing you could have solved all your problems if she had only accepted the gift of immortality."

"If only she would have viewed it as a gift," I muttered. "She was very open to my 'affliction' in the beginning, accepting that I had to feed on others, even encouraging it because she disliked it so much. But soon after our first anniversary, she told me that she would not bear my children and that she would only take me within her sexually during my feedings, which were very rare with her to begin with."

"But why?" she asked. "Surely she knew your relationship would head in that direction. You're immortal."

"She did, but her delusional thoughts and devout Catholic

upbringing had convinced her she had wed a demon. I'll never forget the night she told me that. I was devastated. A thousand times, I tried to sway her to my thinking, and a thousand times, she would only tell me to pray to God and ask that he spare me from being an abomination."

A tear slipped down Korrina's cheek. "Obsidian, that's awful."

"It was awful, and the crazy thing is, no matter what I had to go through in our marriage, I doubt there will ever be a night I would like to forget more than the night I had to bury her. She was my only, despite her hatred of what I was."

Tightening her arms around me, she said, "You have endured so much. I guess I didn't think that you might be a real person. I'm sorry about that. I'm sorry I've been such a bitch to you."

I grinned into her hair, surprised by her apology. I hadn't expected one. "Korrina, I'm not a person. I'm a vampire. You would do well to remember that."

She pulled back to look into my eyes. "Wait a minute. You weren't ever human?"

"No, I was born like this. Just as you and Oswin were born the way you were. True vampires are rare, but not unheard of."

She moved back into the feeding position and shrugged. "You look like a regular vampire to me."

"What does a 'regular' vampire look like?" I asked, smiling at her nonchalance.

Korrina rattled off a short list on her slender fingers. "Pale, ridiculously handsome, sexy as hell, you know, vampire-y in general."

"You think I'm pale?"

Korrina gaped at me. "That's what you got out of all that?"

My smile widened. "Well, I know I'm those other things."

"And so modest, too," she said, rolling her eyes.

I laughed. When she wasn't being a giant pain in my ass, she was quite the charming nymph.

"So, are we finally done with Project Hate Each Other?" she asked.

My lips quirked up. "Why, yes, I do believe we are."

Korrina aimed a truly genuine smile at me. "I'm glad."

That smile was like a jolt of energy to my system. Electric and wild, it shot through my body like a strike of lightning. She was so beautiful, so sexy and voluptuous—she was a fantasy come to life. I found myself unable to think of anything but what she would taste like as she writhed underneath me.

Impulsively, I leaned in, brushing my lips against hers. They were soft, warm, and instantly receptive, a sharp contrast to mine, which were cold and tense. Willing myself to relax, I lapped at her mouth, reveling in the pure indulgence of being with a female who wanted me, who whimpered in need as she pulled me closer to her.

I broke the kiss, staring at her in bewilderment. In all my years, no one had ever wanted me like this. "May I unclothe you, Korrina?" I asked, sure I would wake up from this dream if I didn't act on it.

She nodded and helped me pull her top over her head. The supple breasts that spilled over her bra nearly made me come without even touching her. Words could not accurately describe how exquisite she was.

"Can I see you, too?" she asked meekly.

I didn't answer, just continued to stare, speechless at her perfection. My erection throbbed painfully as I looked her over.

"Obsidian?"

I shook my head to clear it. "I'm sorry? Did you say something?"

She laughed seductively. "Take off your clothes. I want to see you."

Too stunned to speak, I stood and undressed quickly, not wanting to miss a moment of her wriggling her skirt over her hips or the moment her panties joined the matching bra on the nightstand.

When she was completely undressed, she crooked her finger at me. "Come here."

She didn't have to ask me twice. I was back on top of her in a blink of an eye, kissing her as deeply as I could through my fangs. Her hands were everywhere, threaded in my hair, stroking down my chest, slipping around my back, and when I accidentally grazed her center, grabbing my ass. She was ready, and she wanted me, badly. As I followed the line of her vein with my tongue, I could smell the perfume of her eagerness growing stronger every second. It was heaven.

"Fuck me, Obsidian," she purred into my ear. "I want to feel you inside of me."

My cock jumped at her words, and I shuddered. Fuck, she was perfect. She knew exactly what to say to make me forget that we had hated each other ten minutes ago. And for that, I would be eternally grateful. Hate was the furthest thing from my mind.

I sat back on my heels, my fingers trembling as I followed the blush of her skin from her rosy cheeks, to her collarbone, and down to her full breasts. She arched into my hands, my name falling from her perfect mouth in a moan of pleasure. "Korrina, are you sure you want this?" I asked. I had to know for sure. If we took this any further, there would be no turning back.

She slid her hands on top of mine and pressed her breasts into my hands. "I want this."

Without another word, I pushed into her, watching her face intently as it morphed from frustrated want to rapture with every inch I gave her. I was sure it echoed my own. She was so tight, so hot; I didn't think I would last ten seconds inside her.

Korrina writhed against me, her breath coming out in sharp pants. "Obsidian, please … please move."

"Patience, nymph," I told her, eyes squeezed shut as I desperately tried to hold onto my control. "Give me a second."

"Just one," she said quietly. "Then I want you to fuck me while you feed from me."

My eyes flew open. She had bitten her lip hard enough to bring blood. I watched it well up from the tiny cut, forgetting about the building orgasm and the need to make this good for her. All I knew was that I was hungry, so damn hungry for Korrina. I fought against the need until all I could see was red.

Mindless, I dragged her hips up, throwing her legs over my shoulders, nearly bending her in half to sink my teeth into her vein. It was too rough, the bite too savage, but it drove her wild.

"Fuck me," she moaned, over and over.

I did as she commanded. I couldn't stop. I didn't know how. She felt and tasted so good I kept losing myself in the spice of her blood, the scent of her hair, and the feel of her around me. I'd never had a lover like this. There was no doubt of her desire as she bucked against me, digging her nails in my back so hard that I had to pin her arms over her head to keep suction on her neck. She was the picture of want, of need. She wanted everything I gave her and more.

"Obsidian!" she screamed weakly, her body tightening underneath me in orgasm.

Her faded voice brought me out of my trance. I blinked a few times before I realized what I'd done. Quickly, I licked the wounds on her neck to start the healing process and lifted my weight so she could breathe. "I'm sorry, Korrina," I said, pushing her sweaty hair from her face.

She gave me a silly grin. "For what? You're fantastic."

"Fantastic? That may be the nicest thing you've ever said to me." I arched an eyebrow. "How much blood did I take?"

She laughed and wrapped her legs around my waist. "And this is the nicest thing you've ever done for me."

I grinned back at her. "It's not such a chore."

"I should smack you for that, but what you're doing right now is just unnatural." She groaned and used her hips to up the speed of my thrusts. Arching her back in bliss, she muttered, "Obsidian, I'm really, really glad you agreed to be my friend."

"Is that what this is?" I asked. I bit her on the shoulder and enjoyed another pleasured groan for my effort. "Friendly fucking?"

She met my eyes. "Do you want more from me—a relationship?"

Did I want more? Her beauty and kind heart put aside, she had infinitely more to offer me than a human would and her immortality made her a perfect candidate for a life-mate. I honestly couldn't hope for better. 'Better' didn't exist. Still, I wondered. "What could I ever offer you in a relationship, Korrina?"

"Love?"

"Is that something you're looking for with me?"

"Maybe. Is that something you can give me?"

I answered her in the same fashion. "Maybe."

She laughed again. "So, you're saying that it's possible that we might fall in love?"

"That's exactly what I'm saying."

"Well, you're my only neighbor for miles. I like the odds of us ending up together." She rolled herself on top of me with strength I didn't know she had, immediately resuming the sexy movements that were milking me towards an orgasm eight years overdue. "I love fucking you."

The feeling was one hundred percent mutual. The hot vise of her heat had me on the verge of release since the moment I was fully sheathed inside her. I groaned loudly. "Korrina, I can't last much longer."

"Come inside me," she ordered breathlessly.

No sooner than the words left her lips, I was helpless but to obey her, lifting her knees off the mattress with the ferocity of my thrusts. She braced herself on my chest, looking positively etheral as we came together. Her eyes were greener than I'd ever seen them, her face almost alien in its beauty. At that moment, she was the embodiment of sex and desire. And as I came deep inside her, I knew that desire was bringing my cold, dead heart back to life.

"Wow," Korrina gasped, collapsing on top of me. She lifted her head to look at me after a few seconds. "Obsidian, you don't have a heartbeat. Say something, or I'm going to think I've permanently killed you."

I smiled as I stared at the ceiling. "I know you have other offers, but where do I stand in your list of suitors now?"

She leaned up to brush her lips against mine. "Are you kidding? First on the list."

"And how many are on this list?" Before she could answer, I withdrew slightly and pushed back into her.

"Just you," she sighed, pressing her palms into my chest and slowly rocking against the erection that refused to falter.

"Right answer," I said, sitting up and latching on to her nipple, scraping it lightly with my fangs before biting down.

"Obsidian!" She gripped my hair in both hands and kissed me deeply, her pulsating tightness consuming me until I couldn't hold back the yell of her name as I came.

I dropped to the bed with Korrina still clenched tight to my chest. "Are you okay?" I asked.

Tipping her perfect face up to me with a sensual smile, she purred, "Very okay. You?"

I sighed, laughing a bit. "I believe I feel every bit of my one hundred and thirty-two years right now, you succubus."

She laughed and pecked me on the lips. "I thought you did pretty well for someone who is over a hundred years older than me."

"A hundred?" I exclaimed, gaping at her. I covered my eyes with a hand. "Your youthful exuberance will be the death of me."

"Somehow, I think you'll survive." She lifted my hand from my eyes and pulled me towards the edge of the bed. "Come on, old man, let's get you in the shower."

***

I was in lust. Everything about Korrina made me hard for her—the way she shyly tried to cover her breasts as we walked to the adjoining bathroom, the way she leaned over the tub to turn the faucet handles, unknowingly displaying herself to me. Every little thing she did was sexy. Even now, she was utterly oblivious to the torture she was inflicting on me as she bent over the bathtub, her hand under the water flow, testing the temperature. "Korrina, you're killing me," I groaned, barely in control.

Her breath caught as she turned. I must have been quite a sight to her, leaned up in a corner, trembling with restraint, my cock excruciatingly hard for her.

"Obsidian? Are yo—"

I pounced, taking her on the floor like an animal, plunging deep and pounding into her so hard that by the time we'd both orgasmed, we'd slid halfway into the hallway on the bathroom rug. "Fuck, I'm sorry, Korrina," I said, honestly embarrassed by my eagerness. "I really want to treat you better than this."

She kissed me long and slow, carefully avoiding my fangs. "Don't ever apologize for craving me. I want you to want me. I love the way you feel inside me—your cock and your fangs."

"And I love the way you taste," I admitted, nipping at her neck and enjoying the pleasured shudder she gave after. "You taste like heaven."

"This feels like heaven."

"What?" I had to laugh. She thought lying over the threshold on a bathmat was heaven?

"Don't laugh," she said. "It's going to be so hard to leave here."

"The floor?" I asked.

It was her turn to laugh. "No. It will be hard to leave you."

I stood and helped her to her feet, feeling slightly smug because of her words. I'd hoped she'd enjoyed her time here as much as I had. "You know you don't have to go."

A small furrow appeared between her brows. "I will, eventually. Oswin is supposed to come by in the morning. He asked me to breakfast."

For a moment, I was so angry, a film of red covered my eyes. It was as if she'd stabbed me in the heart. I couldn't believe she still intended to keep her date with the wolf. He could not have her. I wouldn't allow it.

She snapped her fingers in front of my face. "Obsidian? Are you okay?"

Her voice broke through the hurricane of rage that was spinning in my mind. With clenched teeth, I answered her. "You have to choose, Korrina. I will not share you with him."

"I have chosen. I'm going to tell him I can't see him anymore."

I backed her up to the wall, kissed her roughly, and growled out, "Call him—now."

"My cell phone … is in the car," she whimpered, her breath shaky against my lips.

In a haze of mist, I disappeared, transporting myself outside to her car as fast as I could. I materialized just long enough to grab the phone out of the console then reappeared in front of Korrina seconds later.

Wide-eyed and trembling, she asked, "Where did you go?"

I held out her phone. "Outside."

Ignoring the phone, she reached out, pressing her fingers to my chest as if to reassure herself that I was really there. She sighed. "You scared the life out of me. How do you do that?"

"No distractions," I said, handing her the phone. Starting right now, Korrina would be mine and no one else's. "First, call the wolf."

BREAKUPS AND BLOODY LIPS

KORRINA

"Obsidian is an enigma," I thought, as I took the phone from him. Every other male I'd been with just wanted me for sex and nothing more. Not him. Even after all of our bickering, even after I'd given myself to him so quickly, he still wanted me. Like, really wanted me. That did remarkable things for my ego.

"Why are you hesitating?" Obsidian asked impatiently. "Are you reluctant to end your affair?"

I rolled my eyes. "It's hardly an affair, Obsidian. We had sex once."

"Twice. You forget about the unrivaled hearing a vampire possesses."

"So I did," I teased, mentally kicking myself for not being honest … and not being quieter.

"Do this for me," he pleaded. "Knowing that he will not be invited back to my property will ease me."

"I will, I promise. I'm just a little nervous. I hate hurting someone's feelings. And Oswin is an especially large, easily pissed off someone."

Frowning, he nodded. "I'll be waiting for you in the shower."

"Thanks."

He stepped into the tub and pulled the curtain closed. "Korrina?"

I stopped scrolling through my contacts. "Yes?"

"Don't take too long. The hot water won't last forever."

Right. I closed the bathroom door and leaned my forehead against the cold wall, dreading the conversation I was about to have.

It only rang once before Oswin picked up. "Hey, darlin'. I was just thinking about you."

With a shaky voice, I said, "Hi, Oswin."

"Are you okay, Korrina? You don't sound right."

"I'm fine. It's just…" God, I really, really, really hated this. "I don't think it's going to work out between us. I—I'm sorry for leading you on."

Oswin sighed deeply. "I wish that the timing would have been right between us. I really do. I liked you a lot."

"I'm sorry, Oswin," I reiterated, feeling like a schmuck. "I really am."

"Well, I guess it was nice knowing you, Korrina."

"And you, Oswin."

I hung up the phone and breathed a massive sigh of relief before I re-opened the bathroom door. Oswin had taken that a lot better than I thought he would. Maybe he was like my other lovers and only wanted me for sex. If that was the case, I was glad I didn't have to go through the heartbreak of finding out the hard way.

Feeling much better about the situation, I put my cell phone on the sink and slid back the curtain to join Obsidian, only to stop suddenly when I saw his wet, naked body. I didn't think anybody had ever looked as striking as he did as he washed the shampoo from his hair. The sudsy water sluiced down his chest and into the dark curls around his erection, making it almost impossible not to worship what he was offering.

His eyes popped open. "Korrina, you look—"

"I look hungry," I answered for him.

He smirked. "That's exactly what I was going to say." Holding his arms out, he smiled a fanged grin. "Care for anything you see here?"

Stepping into the tub, I stroked his hard length. "As a matter of fact, I do see something that I like." I sank to my knees, slowly taking him into my mouth, never breaking eye contact.

"Fuck, Korrina," he hissed sharply, his muscles tensing as he braced his arms on two walls.

Encouraged, I continued my steady rhythm, watching every emotion that crossed his face until he closed his eyes, turned his face skyward, and roared his release. After a few seconds, he brought his gaze back to mine and helped me to my feet. Lightning fast, he spun me to face the curtain, pulling my body tight against his. He was impossibly hard for someone who had already had a handful of orgasms in the last thirty minutes.

"I have a plan," he whispered in my ear.

A frisson of fear raced through me, speeding up my heart rate. "What kind of plan?" I asked, willing myself not to beg for his bite.

Instead of answering me, he nudged my head to the side and ran his nose across my skin, breathing in my scent, then scraped his blunt teeth from my neck to my shoulder. "One that has multiple steps."

Snaking his arm around my ribs, he crushed me to his body and slid a slick, soapy hand between my legs. I sighed and rested the back of my head on his chest. He increased the pressure of his fingers, coaxing his name from my lips.

"I will never tire of hearing the way you say my name," he murmured in my ear, so low I almost didn't hear it over the spray of the shower and my own pounding heart.

Unable to articulate anything more than sounds of pleasure as he moved his fingers in a tight, delicious circle, I mumbled incoherently in response.

"Come for me," he ordered in a low voice, obviously expecting complete compliance.

I was powerless to deny his demands, crying out almost

instantly and shuddering against his hard chest, the mind-blowing, full-body orgasm making me sag in his firm grip. Dazed, I barely felt the smile against my neck before he placed a light kiss on the top of my wet head, turned off the shower, and lifted me into his arms.

"What are you doing?" I asked. "I'm not done."

"Oh, you're done," he insisted.

I arched an eyebrow. "I am?"

He gave me a fanged smile that could only be interpreted as 'I'm going to eat you up in every way imaginable'. "The shower will keep, Korrina. It's time to begin step one of my plan."

***

Step one of Obsidian's plan was sex, a lot of sex. More sex than I'd had in a whole year sex. We did the deed in his bed, got hot and heavy against two of his bedroom's walls, did the not so horizontal mambo on his granite kitchen countertop, and even got busy on the thick grass just past his back porch. Every part of my body was blissfully sore, and I couldn't have been happier about it.

Obsidian seemed pretty happy about it, too. He couldn't keep his hands off of me … literally. Whenever we were within touching distance, there was always a possessive hand on the back of my neck or an arm around my waist. It was as if he was magnetically drawn to me. Either that, or he was planning on locking me in the basement when I tried to leave.

Whatever the reason, I was enjoying being with him. He was weird, in a good way, and a little old-fashioned. He said and did things that made me giggle. And it didn't hurt that he was breathtakingly beautiful to look at. I couldn't get enough of his lean, muscular body or his square jaw, aristocratic nose, or the sharp, amber eyes that kept cutting toward me. He was irresistible, bringing me to the edge of obsession. I couldn't stop the thoughts of his mouth, his cock, and especially his fangs. His bite was so damn addictive.

Obsidian opened an eye. "You're making me nervous, Korrina."

I smiled, glad I had a reason to look at him without feeling like a stalker. "How?"

"I can feel you staring at me."

"Oh, I didn't realize I was staring?"

He gave me a wildly exasperated look and laughed. "Korrina!"

Laying back on my pillow, I looked away from him. "Forgive me, I can't … I mean, it's hard to not look at you."

He snorted. "It is?"

"I want you," I told him. "I want you so bad that I can barely stand it. You have no idea what it's like wanting you like this all the time."

Obsidian pulled me on top of him and skimmed his hands down my bare hips. "I have some idea."

I ground myself against his growing erection. "You do?"

"Ye—" he started, stopping short when I took his face in my hands and kissed him—hard, so hard I cut his lip on his fang.

"I'm sorry," I said, frantically trying to untie the knot on his pajama pants. "I just need you inside me. Like, right now."

His face was emotionless as he pulled my hands from his pants. "Stop, Korrina."

I sat back on my knees. "What's wrong?"

"Did you make my lip bleed to drink my blood?"

Obsidian's cold, formal voice startled me. I recoiled from it. "Why on Earth would I do that?"

His angry expression fell. Sitting up, he took my hand and spoke calmly. "Korrina, in about five or ten minutes, you're going to feel really euphoric … and very horny."

"Why?" I asked. "What's going on?"

He sighed. "Vampires have certain enzymes in their blood. Its effect is similar to the human's ecstasy drug."

"Are you telling me your blood is a drug?" I screeched.

"Yes! I thought you knew! Every nymph does. Every normal one, anyway."

I shot him a scathing look.

"Let me rephrase that. What I meant was that any nymph that has been around the block knows about it. It's one of the reasons I distrusted you so much when we met."

"You thought I'd offer myself up in exchange for your blood?"

"I didn't know you as I do now, Korrina.

"How long is it going to last?" I asked, my voice a thousand times steadier than my mind.

"You didn't take too much. It probably won't affect you for more than twenty minutes, but it's going to be an intense twenty minutes."

I nodded. "Will it show up in a drug test or anything?"

His brow furrowed. "Why would you ask that?"

I bit my lip. I was going to have to tell him about my conviction. But how? How could I convince him that I wouldn't just fuck anyone anywhere when I'd just fucked him and Oswin? Nymph or not, I was starting to feel a little ashamed by my need for sex. It made me make rash decisions. It made me weak.

"Look, Obsidian, I should have told you before. I was cast out of Meadowbrook as punishment for too many arrests. If I get into trouble again, they could send me to the Bureau's prison."

His eyes hardened. "You're on parole?"

Tears sprang to my eyes. "Of a sort."

62

"You told me you weren't a prostitute, Korrina." His voice was harsh and as frigid as ice.

"I'm no—" I clenched my teeth together as a wave of pure bliss roiled through my body.

Obsidian rolled me to my back and hovered over me with black, emotionless eyes. "Korrina, I'll fuck you now, but after tonight, I don't want you to speak to me. I don't want you to come back to my home. I just want you to leave me be."

I was astonished at the vehemence in his tone. I couldn't understand why he was so angry. All I felt was him, hard and pressed so deliciously against me. It felt like nothing I'd ever felt before, and I wanted it like nothing I'd desired before. I was raw and open and ready.

Another wave of pure lust shot through me, and I cried out, arching against his huge erection. "Please, Obsidian. Please."

Unmoved, he asked. "Did you hear what I said, Korrina?"

I writhed against his body, desperately seeking the pleasure I know he could give me. I was beyond comprehension. All I knew was a stark need. All I could see was him inside me, quenching this terrible thirst before it consumed me. And when I finally felt him move roughly into me, I saw nothing else.

***

The next morning, I woke up in my bed with a very foggy memory of the night before and no recollection of how I got home.

I sat up groggily and looked around. Everything seemed perfectly normal, except for my folded clothes on the foot of the bed and a parchment envelope, just like the one Obsidian had sent the dinner invitation in, on my nightstand. A sense of foreboding struck me when I looked at that envelope. What had happened last night? Something bad, I suspected.

The note inside confirmed my fears. I read the lines over and over, trying to make sense of them.

I thought you were different.

I was a fool.

A sharp pain tore across my chest as the inevitable panic settled in, and I pressed my hand to my heart. It felt as if it had cracked in two. I wrapped my arms around myself and rocked, trying to remember how to breathe. Did I love Obsidian? Was that why this hurt so bad?

I knew the answer. If I didn't love him, it wouldn't hurt.

***

The wait until dusk nearly killed me. I paced back in forth across the living room for hours. I plotted out every word I would say to him. And I prayed. I prayed like I'd never prayed before. Whatever it took, I would do. I had to make things right with Obsidian. It was a bone-deep need inside of me. He was the one. I could feel it all the way from the top of my head to the tips of my toes. All this time I'd thought it was Solon that sent me here. But it wasn't my uncle that brought me to Goshen. It was fate.

The moment the sun slipped out of sight, I ran to Obsidian's house. Not surprisingly, the trees were full of sorrow for me. They reached to console me as I ran through them and into his yard, but I didn't acknowledge them. I only had eyes for Obsidian.

I found him on the porch, wearing a grim expression when I broke through the tree line. "Why are you here, Korrina?" he asked.

"I want to know what happened between us last night," I answered, though there was so much contempt in his tone, I had to lock my knees to keep myself from stepping back into the safety of the trees.

He smirked nastily. "You don't remember telling me about your arrest record?"

I shook my head and stared at the ground. "I should have told you sooner."

"Just go," he said wearily. "You're no different than any of the rest of them."

My head shot up. "That's not fair. I'm not like them."

"Oh no?" He sped down the stairs to me in half a second. "Were those arrests a mistake? Are you saying that you didn't fuck those males?"

I wanted to slap the smirk off his face. "Fuck you, Obsidian. You've never had any one night stands?"

"Not until I met your kind," he said scathingly. "Now leave my property before I call the Bureau and tell them that you're harassing me."

I blinked away the tears forming in my eyes. "Please, Obsidian. Don't do this. I love you."

"Hold your tongue, nymph," he scoffed. "You only love what I am and what I can do to you—nothing more."

"That's not true. I swear it!"

Ignoring me, he turned to mist and disappeared without another word.

"Obsidian!" I cried out, collapsing onto my knees in agony, my heart broken into a million pieces.

***

Days passed before my tears dried up. But I was sure that had more to do with the store running out of tissues than it did with me being over Obsidian.

Every single day, I woke up painfully aware that I lived in a house belonging to a male that despised me, while I loved him to my very core. I felt like a ghost in his house—a lost soul desperately trying to find a way out of this Hell and back to him. It couldn't be over between us already. I just needed to keep it together long enough for him to get over his anger and let me explain.

That was a good idea in theory, but it wasn't so great in

reality. After several more days of no contact from Obsidian, I had a significant breakdown. It all started with an innocent Bougainvillea leaf falling into my glass of lemonade. At first, I sat there, staring at the fuchsia leaf bobbing merrily on top of the ice. Then I backhanded it off the table in a fit of rage.

With an angry scream of fury, I walked purposefully to the shed and grabbed my garden shears. Marching back, I focused all of my aggression on cutting the thorny, flowering vines down. Over and over, I whacked at the vines until there was nothing left but the stumps and mountains of wasted flowers around me. I didn't care that my arms were stinging and covered in scrapes and scratches. I didn't care that the trees around me shrunk back in fear as they whispered soothing words to me. I just wanted everything to stop, the pain, the loneliness—the hurt. It all had to stop. Collapsing in exhaustion, I fell onto the nearest pile of debris and cried, letting the darkness of my misery steal over me without a care.

BURNING UP WITH PASSION
OBSIDIAN

In all of my one hundred and thirty-two years, I doubt I have ever been as torn about something as I'd been over Korrina. I ached for her. I craved her. It was maddening.

Of course, I wasn't naive enough to think we could ever have anything between us. The whole damn thing was so fucking fruitless. I kept trying to explain that rationale to my dick, but he wasn't having any of it. He wanted her back—now.

And what made things so much worse was that I knew I had made a mockery of what could have been between us. A fool could have seen how genuinely distraught Korrina was on the night I asked her to leave my property. When I saw her collapse to the dirt and cry out my name, I stayed close by, even trying to follow her through the woods as she picked herself off the ground to make her way back home, but the trees blocked my entry. I could only listen as her cries became softer and softer the farther she traveled away.

The knowledge that my pride had done that to her killed me, and for a few days, she gave me no reprieve from her endless crying. I couldn't complain. I deserved every second of the regret and shame I felt and would continue to feel until I worked up the nerve to beg her forgiveness.

***

At half-past five, on Sunday, she gave me no choice. I awakened from my death sleep with a start, jumping out of bed, and slinging back the curtain, ready to go to Korrina, regardless of the sun's ability to kill me. Her abnormally harsh voice filled the woods around me as she screamed out in rage and pain. What was happening? I yelled as the sun's weak rays hit my stomach and jumped back into the shadows of my bedroom. I could see from my position that the trees were still blocking the shortest path to her, their branches braided together in a twenty-foot-tall privacy fence. Fuck. I'd have to go the long way around. This was going to hurt ... a lot.

With a battle cry, I ran out of my front door at full speed, not stopping until I found Korrina in the backyard laying in a bed of thorns and vines, an open pair of gardening shears perched dangerously above her throat. Taking an agonizing second to move the shears and check her over for injuries, I gritted my teeth against the intense burning and picked her up to carry her in the house. She seemed barely conscious, only moaning when I shifted her weight to open the door. I ran through the kitchen to the hallway, the only room I knew had no windows and collapsed with her in my arms. "You're safe, Korrina. I've got you. I'm right here."

Her eyes fluttered open. "I can't see anything."

"We're in the hallway. It's daytime," I said, pushing her sweaty, matted hair back from her face.

"Daytime?" she asked, looking confused. A second later, her eyes opened wide when she realized what was happening. "Obsidian, are you hurt?"

"Burned, but I will heal soon enough. When your screaming woke me, I panicked. What happened out there?"

"Oh my God. This isn't happening," she moaned, gingerly trying to leave my lap without hurting me.

"What isn't?" I asked, bewildered at her mortified expression.

Slowly, she felt around the floor until she found the opposite wall and sat down, looking positively terrified as she hugged her knees to her chest. "Obsidian, I'm not hurt. I just kind of ... lost it."

"Lost it? Korrina, are you telling me I risked turning myself to ash to save you from a hissy fit?"

She squinted her eyes closed and made herself small against the wall, obviously expecting the worst. "Yes?"

I barked out a laugh and sagged against the wall. "Oh, this is priceless."

Her eyes popped open. "You're not mad?"

"Only at myself. When I heard you screaming, all I could think of was the abominable treatment you received from me. I couldn't let anything else happen to you, not before ..." I trailed off and moved to her, gritting my teeth against the pain of the burnt flesh on my shoulder knitting back together. Thank God, she couldn't see me in this state. "Korrina, I owe you an apology."

She shook her head resolutely. "No, you really don't."

"Of course I do," I argued, taken aback by the finality in her words. "How could I not?"

"Obsidian, in less than two weeks, I kept secrets from you, used you for sex, destroyed God knows how old plants around the gazebo in a fit of insanity, and got you beat up by a werewolf. And on top of all that, I distinctly remember you warning me to keep it in mind that you aren't a person. I didn't listen. I expected you ..." She sighed. "I don't know what I expected."

It was official. She was the saintliest nymph on the planet. "You didn't use me for sex any more than I used you, Korrina, and as far as the wolf and plants go, I deserved that and better for the way I treated you. I know what you expected. You expected me to be decent."

"Don't justify my actions, Obsidian. Just don't. I'm not in Goshen on holiday. I'm here because I can't stay out of trouble. I don't deserve apologies, or even happiness, after the lives I've manipulated for my gain."

I grinned. "Manipulated for your gain? Who are you? Lex Luther?"

She pouted. "Don't make fun of me."

"I'm not. I'm just trying to make you understand that whatever you've done, it can't be as bad as you're making it out to be. The proof is that you're not in the Bureau's prison."

"Obsidian, please." Growling with irritation, she lifted herself from the floor and found the light switch, flipping it up. "I—" She stared aghast at my burned skin. "Why didn't you tell me it was this bad?"

"I didn't want to frighten you," I said, turning my monstrous appearance away from her gaze. "It will heal when I feed."

"Then, do it," she urged, holding her wrist in front of my nose. "I can't bear for you to be in pain because of me—again."

I pressed a kiss to her tiny wrist, reluctant to hurt her. In the back of my mind, I knew how wrong it was to use Korrina for her blood. It was selfish, a despicable thing to do when she was blaming herself for my mistakes. But the vampire in me wanted to take what she so willingly offered. Not only would it save me from hypnotizing a human into forgetting that a burn victim mauled them like a hungry animal, but it was also infinitely safer than risking going out into the open while I was at my weakest. There wasn't a choice. It seemed there'd never be a choice with Korrina. It was all of her or nothing.

***

After dark, I set out to Meadowbrook. It was beyond tiresome to go to the nymph's safe haven, but it was necessary. I needed answers, and my oldest friend, Solon, had them. He rented the house for Korrina so he would know precisely what Korrina's past entailed.

I pulled into Solon's small driveway a little after two in the morning. I didn't bother calling first. He'd know what I was after the moment he saw me. Or, at least, I thought he would. I wasn't expecting the punch to the face that I got when I rang the doorbell.

Clad in plaid button up pajamas, he was spitting mad with his fists balled up. It would have been comical—if he hadn't kept trying to swing at me. "What the hell, Solon?"

"Why the fuck did you do that to my niece?" he yelled. "She hasn't stopped crying for days!"

"Korrina is your niece?" I asked. I'd never seen him so worked up.

"She's my favorite niece, asshole! What the fuck were you thinking?"

He came at me again. "Solon! Stop!" I yelled, blocking his blows. "Believe me, I didn't want to hurt her. She lied to me about being a prostitute then told me the truth after she'd taken my blood."

He stopped suddenly, looking murderous. "Prostitute? Did you just call my niece a fucking prostitute? And did you say you gave her your blood?" He walked toward me slowly, and I started backing away. I didn't know what he was capable of. "I sent Korrina to you because I thought I could trust you, Obsidian. She was vulnerable and unused to living alone. I thought you'd be a good match for her."

"A match?" I asked incredulously. "You knew I was still in mourning, Solon."

"Mourning? Are you fucking kidding me? Edith drove you insane. She couldn't have been more wrong for you. You knew that. If you weren't such a selfish asshole, you would have left her fifty years ago!" He shook his head. "Look, I know why you came here, and the answer is no. She's never been with a vampire or a John. She's only been caught having public sex with local males. She didn't have anywhere else to take them. You know how hard celibacy can be for a young nymph, especially with an overbearing family like she has. I pitied her ... and you. It would have been a blessing for both of you if you weren't such a fucking idiot."

"Why am I an idiot?" I asked defensively.

"Are you with Korrina right now?"

He was right. I was an idiot. I'd become so jaded; I wouldn't listen to her when she tried to tell me the truth. "I have to go."

"It's too late. You'll never make it back before the sun comes up. Come on in. I'll go get the blackout curtains out of the linen closet."

I followed him inside. "I hope you're not right, Solon."

"About what?"

"I hope it's not too late.

"When did you last see her?"

"A few hours ago. She's in torment because of me, Solon."

"No shit." He handed me his phone. "Call her now, moron. Tell her you love her … before I fucking stake you for breaking her heart."

Korrina answered on the fourth ring. "Hello? Uncle Solon?"

"It's Obsidian."

She was silent for a moment. "What are you doing at my uncle's house? Is everything okay?"

Now that I had her on the line, I didn't know what I should say. I love you? I'm a jackass? Please don't fuck anyone else or it will rip my heart out? I wasn't sure how to start.

"Are you there? Obsidian?"

"Sorry, yes. Solon is one of my oldest friends. I came here for advice. Korrina, listen. I've been an idiot. I know now that I didn't have any reason to distrust you. I'm begging you to forgive me for my mistakes."

"I forgave you the second I read the note." Her voice was soft, almost a whisper. "But, Obsidian, I've had a lot of time to think this over, and I don't think we should be together. We make each other crazy. We constantly fight. If we're capable of hurting each other so easily, I don't think we're going to work."

"Please, give me another chance," I begged. "Korrina, please. I promise it will be different. I'll be different."

She sighed. "I'm sorry, Obsidian. I have to go."

The connection clicked off, and so did my sanity. I took off running without a word to Solon. It would take only an hour or so to travel on foot if I didn't attract any unwanted attention. I had to get to Korrina now.

Korrina's bedroom light was still on as I sped onto her porch. I glanced at the horizon. There wasn't much time before daybreak. I knocked hard on the door and waited, praying she would answer, while I stared at the wreckage caused by my fight with Oswin. I would fix that. I would fix all of this.

"Who is it?" I heard her sweet voice say from somewhere above me.

"Open the door, Korrina. I have something that needs to be said before you shut me out of your life."

"Obsidian?"

Walking out into the driveway, I looked up at the balcony. There she stood, ethereally beautiful in the gauzy white nightgown she wore. It would have taken my breath away if I had to breathe at all.

"What are you doing here?" she asked, frowning as she leaned over the railing to look down at me.

"Can I come up?"

"Yes," she said hesitantly.

With an uncustomary show of strength, I leaped up over the railing. "Thank you for seeing me. There isn't much time before the sunrise."

"How did you get here so fast? You were three hours away."

"I ran."

She furrowed her brow. "Come inside."

I followed her into her bedroom, glad to see that she'd restored every piece of my parent's furniture to perfection. I shouldn't have been surprised. Everything she touched, she made better.

"Why did you run here?" she asked, pointing to the bedside chair.

Ignoring the chair, I fell to my knees. "I think I might love you, Korrina. Marry me."

She shook her head. "I think you should start going over what you're going to say before you say it, Obsidian. You want me to marry you because you think that you might love me? Are you joking?"

In earnest, I told her, "I'm serious, Korrina. I don't want anyone else but you."

She paced across the room, avoiding my glance. "I need time away from you, Obsidian. Even if I disregard your acid tongue, I'm not sure I can go through another fight."

Sighing, I got to my feet and stepped in her path. "How will you ever, if I am not in your life?"

She shook her head again. "I don't know."

"Let me prove myself worthy of your love, Korrina. Please, have mercy on me."

Tears slipped down her cheeks as she reached to run her fingers through my hair. "Obsidian, please, don't hurt me again."

"Never," I promised, burying my face into her neck and breathing her in.

"I hope that's true," she murmured.

I took her in my arms and kissed her. "Spend the evening with me tonight, my love."

Pulling away, she said, "I can't. I have a dinner date with a friend tonight."

"With a male friend?"

She looked me square in the eye. "Yes, and I'm not canceling. I still think we need time apart."

"So you can get cozy with another male?"

"This is not about sex."

I gave her an incredulous look. "Then what is it about?"

"Obsidian, you're making this into a bigger deal than it is."

Giving in, I stepped closer to her body, forcing her to hold on to my biceps or lose her balance. "You want me to woo you, don't you?"

It took her two tries to speak. "Doesn't every female want to be wooed?"

"How shall I start?" I asked, placing small kisses along her jaw.

A very feminine sigh fell from her lips. "Well, it has been a few days since…"

I didn't let her finish. I lifted her into my arms and placed her gently on the bed. "Let me make love to you."

Her eyes twinkled in merriment. "Um … Obsidian?"

"Korrina?" I asked, uncertain at her reaction.

"I was going to ask if you could check the high shelves for dust."

I gaped at her. "Are you serious?"

She sobered. "Yes."

"You will truly be the death of me," I moaned, looking down at my erection.

Laughing, she sat up. "You keep saying that, and yet, you're still here."

"You make an excellent point, as usual," I said, glancing out the balcony doors at the sky beginning to pinken on the horizon. I was out of time. "Love, I have to get going if I'm going to make it home before light. Can you ask the trees to unblock my path home?"

Her brows lifted. "They blocked you?"

I sat next to her, hugged her to my chest, and pressed my lips to the top of her head. "It was deserved."

She pursed her lips together and seemed to concentrate intently for a moment. "Okay, they've agreed to move."

I bent my head and kissed her with every ounce of passion I had for her. "Don't give up on me. I love you, Korrina."

Though she didn't say anything when I pulled away, I could feel her eyes on me as I jumped over the balcony railing and ran out of sight.

BREAKING ALL THE RULES
KORRINA

October 15th

Journal, when I said that Obsidian needed medication, I should have been clearer. He needs a truckload of medication. He wants to marry me now? What. The. Hell? A week ago, he never wanted to see me again. Obviously, he's confused ... and possibly a freaking psycho, and I'm the moron that still wants him—craves him. I'm so close to giving in, I can practically taste the salt of his skin, smell the scent of his hair. The only thing keeping me in this room are the questions I can't ignore. How does he know Uncle Solon, and what are they cooking up together?

K

Ten minutes ago, I would have said that there was nothing Obsidian could ever say to make me feel anything for him again. Him showing up at my balcony this morning changed all of that. The romantic in me was like a pig in mud. I'd nearly swooned when he kissed me and would have gladly said yes to his proposal if my logical side wasn't screaming at me to distrust him. Damn, I wanted to trust him—I wanted to trust him all night long.

Okay, maybe it might be a good idea to get away from him for a little while. Even though we were half a mile away, he was still too close, and it had been way, way too long since we'd been together. When it came to Obsidian Raines, there wasn't enough rationality in the world to make me reject him. I was smitten.

***

To take my mind off of wanting Obsidian, I focused on the crippling guilt I felt for making another date with Oswin the day before. My trip to the local Dairy Queen had started out innocently enough—until I sensed he was near. It didn't take long to spot him. His keen eyes found mine as soon as I walked in the door. No doubt he knew I was there long before I knew he was.

I smiled and waved, and though I loathed to do it after the way I broke things off, I decided I had to do the polite thing and visit his table. I owed him that much courtesy.

"Hi, Korrina," Oswin said, standing up to greet me with a broad, friendly grin and a bear hug.

Every eye at the table turned to me the second he spoke my name. He had apparently told his three friends about me. "Hi, Oswin." I inclined my head to the human men. "Hi, guys."

One of the men whistled low. "Oswin, for once you didn't lie. She is una mujer muy hermosa. Too bad she dumped your ass!"

"Shut up, Javier. You couldn't keep a woman like her for ten seconds, much less for an entire date."

The cheeky wink Oswin gave me made me blush, but I still breathed an inward sigh of relief. I'd hoped that he hadn't told his friends that we'd had sex. Deep down, I guess I knew he wouldn't. He was more of a gentle-male than that. He'd never hurt me … well, emotionally. Hell, he even tried to warn me about Obsidian. If I would have listened, I could have saved myself a lot of heartaches and would probably be settled with a nice, respectable Alpha wolf by now.

"I just wanted to say 'hello'," I told him. "I'll let you guys get back to your lunch." I turned to go order my Blizzard and was surprised to see Oswin following me to the register. He gently pulled me to the side, out of view of his friends.

"Korrina, what's going on? You don't seem like yourself today."

Traitorous tears popped up in my eyes, prompting Oswin to put his arms around me. "Whatever has happened, I want to know, but not here. Can I come to see you tomorrow? I'll bring the supplies to fix the porch while I'm there."

Resting my head on his chest, I squeezed his middle. "Thank you, Oswin. That would be really great." What else could I do? I couldn't, no, wouldn't refuse his company. I was beyond desperate to have a friend in my life.

"It's my pleasure, darlin'. See you about seven?"

"Sounds good. I'll go to the store and get something fancy for dinner."

He kissed me tenderly on the forehead. "I'm really looking forward to it."

***

With every intention of buying a rack of ribs, a couple chickens, and maybe, a side of beef, I found myself in the grocery store parking lot the next day. But try as I might, I couldn't seem to make myself get out of the car. Every time I thought of Oswin coming to my house, I started to hyperventilate. I had to call this off. At the very least, I had to switch locations. I couldn't flaunt my friendship with him in front of Obsidian. Not with our history and his marriage proposal on the table.

Mind made up, I scrolled through my contacts, tapping on Oswin's name and praying it would go to voicemail because I was a big fat chicken.

He answered after half a ring. "Hey, darlin'."

"Hey, yourself. I just have a quick question for you."

"No, I have no known food allergies, and gluten is fine by me."

I laughed at his easy humor, but secretly wished I could feel half as lighthearted as Oswin. "That's not quite what I wanted to know."

"Okay, then. What's up?"

"Do you think it would be okay if we go out to dinner? I don't really feel like cooking tonight."

"Is that all? Sure thing, baby doll. You know, when I saw your number, I thought you were calling to cancel on me again."

I grimaced. Of course, he did. "Uh, no, just a little cabin fever, that's all. I could meet you halfway, or I could come to you?"

"I would love to show you around Thomasville, but that's a really long ride. I don't feel good about you driving home for two and a half hours in the dark."

I leaned my forehead on the steering wheel. What I was thinking was wrong. So. Damn. Wrong. And against my probation. But his throaty chuckles sped up my heartbeat, and I wanted to spend some time with someone other than Obsidian just for clarity's sake, so I straightened and said, "I could bring an overnight bag."

"Even better. How soon can you be here?"

"Three hours? Maybe less?"

"Good. I'll text you the directions. And Korrina?"

"Yes?"

"I can't wait to see you."

"Me too."

I hit the end button on my cell and just stared at it. Was I really going to do this? Yes, of course, I was because I was a glutton for punishment and a terrible would-be wife.

Feeling like the biggest slut on the planet, I pulled out of the parking lot and broke the speed limit the entire way home. No doubt, to try to outrun the guilt that was already plaguing me.

***

The drive to Oswin's house felt like it took an eternity. My paranoia made it ten times worse. For most of the trip, I obsessed on whether or not Obsidian had overheard me packing and leaving. And while I rationalized that I hadn't promised Obsidian anything—except to give him another chance—and that we didn't have an exclusive relationship, I still worried.

Oswin lived down a long dirt road, and with his super hearing, he probably heard my little car bumping its way down it a mile away. I found him waiting expectantly on the porch when I finally pulled into the driveway of a small, freshly painted shotgun house. Just as tall, blond, and handsome as I remembered him, he hurried to open my car door.

"There she is," he drawled, grinning a toothy smile.

I blushed like a schoolgirl. "Hi."

Grabbing my bag out of the backseat before I could get it, he offered me his other arm. "I'm glad you're here, darlin'. Let me show you where you'll be sleeping."

Suddenly awkward, I climbed the porch steps with Oswin and tried to make small talk. "Your house is beau—" I stopped short, surprised by the two lanky, brunette females that stepped onto the porch right behind us. With their cutoff jeans, halter tops, and flip-flops, I didn't think they were selling Avon.

The shorter one of the two spoke up with a sneer aimed at me. "Aren't you going to introduce us?"

In one swift movement, Oswin shoved me behind him and faced the two. "Ladies, don't go making trouble for yourselves. Just go on home."

The taller, skankier one spoke up. "We just wanted to meet the whore that made you a traitor to your race."

Oswin didn't dignify them with a response. He merely pulled out a cell phone, pressed a button, and within seconds, two heavily armed males walked up to the females and dragged them bodily away, both of them screaming at the top of their lungs. Oswin, seemingly nonplussed at the spectacle, shuffled me inside and locked the door behind him. He grinned as he turned around to my dumbfounded expression. "You'll catch a fly like that."

I snapped my jaw shut and gave him a withering look. "Uh, no offense, Oswin, but what the fuck was that?"

"None taken. That was just a couple of wolves who are having a hard time handling rejection. They're upset with me because I didn't seek either one of them out as a mate. They aren't the only ones, either."

That got my attention. "Am I in danger here? How many are we talking?"

He held his hands up. "Whoa! Don't get carried away. It's not that many—eleven or twelve, at most." Seeing the look of horror on my face, he sighed, defeated. "Look, maybe I've upset a few females, but I'll be damned if I'm going to spend the rest of my life with someone who didn't spare me a second glance until the night I won Alpha. Would you, if you were in my position?"

I didn't have to think that one over for a second. "Definitely not. How can you stand it?"

Grinning again, he took my hand and led me from the living room into the kitchen. "Well, they've only recently started being so vocal about it. If I'm not mistaken, I believe it started the day I came home smelling of sex and nymph."

The growl in those last words made me blush down to my toes. Oswin was ridiculously smooth. He knew just how to lure his prey into a false sense of security. I didn't stand a chance.

"B-but you have armed guards outside, Oswin," I stuttered. "I don't think vocal is the word I would use in this situation."

He pulled me into his arms. "Relax, Korrina. It's just a scare tactic to keep them at bay. Some of the females are prone to violence. I don't want to hurt them in a fight."

"Is it because I'm a nymph. Do they not approve of our kind?"

"Your species is irrelevant. They just know that they could never compete with you. Wolves, especially female wolves, have a tendency to be jealous of nicer, prettier potential mates."

"Mates? What? They think I'm going to be the next Alpha female?"

He laughed. "That's exactly what they think."

Cue the awkward silence.

Taking my hand, he led me to the next room. "Are you

familiar with this style of house, Korrina?"

I furrowed my brows. What an odd question to ask. "Not really. Just that they're pretty popular in the south."

He examined the molding intently before he turned those bottomless blue-green eyes on me. "Shotgun houses only have one bedroom."

I grinned. I couldn't help it. This shy side of Oswin was so adorable. "It's no big deal," I told him. "I promise; I can keep my hands to myself."

"So can I," he said, obviously relieved I wasn't upset. "The last thing I want to do is pressure you. If you aren't ready, I can wait as long as you need me to."

Scratch that adorable thought. He was perfect. And he would never treat me the way Obsidian had treated me.

"This is great, Oswin, but I don't want to put you out or make you uncomfortable. I can sleep on the couch."

"Don't be ridiculous. No guest of mine is going to sleep on the sofa. Plus, I have a hunch that you'll be real nice to cuddle up to. It gets a little chilly in here at night."

"Okay, now that that is settled, how do you plan on keeping me entertained while I'm here?" I smiled expectantly at him.

"Hmmm … let's see. We could go to this little Italian place I know. Of course, when I say little Italian place, I mean a franchised pizza chain in a strip mall. That's about all we've got around here."

"Sounds good. Maybe we could watch a movie after?"

"Perfect," he said, unbuttoning his blue work shirt. He put my overnight bag on the dresser and started pulling off his shirt. "Just let me get out of these work clothes and take a quick shower."

I put my hand in front of my eyes. There was no need for that kind of temptation this early in the day. It was going to be a long enough night as it was. "Uh, I'll be in the living room looking through your books and making wild assumptions of what your character is like based solely on what's on the shelves."

He snickered and stepped out of his jeans. "You do that. I'm interested to hear what you come up with."

Nodding, I lingered a second longer than I had to. I just wanted a little peek at him in his boxer briefs. I opened my fingers slightly. Yep, still smoking hot. Sleeping next to him was going to be torture.

His voice gained a predatory tone. "I like that look, Korrina. It gives a male hope."

A nervous giggle escaped me. "I'm leaving now."

Practically running through the kitchen, I made my way to the safety of the living room and leaned my back on the first wall I came to, closing my eyes tightly to try to calm myself. The farther I was away from him, the better. My body knew the pleasure he could bring me, and just hearing the water running and remembering how it looked as it fell down his tan skin made me ache to have him inside me.

SPARE THE ROD, SPOIL THE NYMPH

KORRINA

October 16th

Only the saddest of creatures would be fervently writing in her journal while a naked, willing werewolf was in the next room. I'm a nymph, for Pete's sake. I should be in there doing what we both know I came to do. What is wrong with me? Apparently, a lot.

K

When I heard Oswin turn on the shower, I tucked my journal back in my purse and forced myself forward to look at the titles on Oswin's woefully small bookcase. Once there, I stopped still. The Bronte sisters, Oscar Wilde, William Thackeray—it was all Victorian literature. The second shelf was even more of a surprise. Box sets of Ursula K. Le Guin and JK Rowling novels stood proudly displayed between a set of intricately carved wolf-shaped bookends. I expected him to read Stephen King or James Patterson, but this could be my own bookcase.

Sitting down on the couch in astonishment, I shook my head. The Alpha of the Thomasville pack was a huge mystery. I just couldn't figure him out. Why would he live in this modest house, but wear thousand dollar suits? It was evident that he had money by him having security guards and a shiny new pickup truck out in the driveway. And what was going on with his personality? It was completely different. He had been assertive to the point of controlling the last time we'd seen each other, and now he was being gentle as a lamb while reading Sense and Sensibility? Something didn't fit, but I just couldn't put my finger on it.

As soon as he emerged from behind the shower curtain, I confronted him with my paranoia. "What's the deal? Are you some kind of serial killer or what?"

He stepped out onto the bath mat, looking alarmed. "What the hell did you find out there? I thought, for sure, I put away the rope and shovel before you got here."

I rolled my eyes. "You're a walking contradiction, Oswin. You have money, but you live modestly. You like Victorian literature, which is way, way against the tough guy code, and you are so a tough guy. On top of all that, you're acting like Prince Charming in a Disney film. It's a complete one-eighty from the way you were before."

He wrapped a towel around his waist and sighed. "I can explain."

Following him out of the bathroom, I sat on his bed and mentally prepared myself for the worst. "All right, I'm ready. Hit me with it."

The corners of his mouth twitched. "Okay, well, first, living modestly is an excellent way to stay wealthy. Or so I've been told. Second, this is where I grew up. I've never wanted to live anywhere else."

"What about the Austen?" I asked, arching my brow. "What possible reason could you give me for that?"

He sat next to me and took my face into his rough hands, smiling and shaking his head a little as he gazed into my eyes. "Korrina, you're kind of adorable."

I grinned. "Funny, I was just thinking the same about you."

He burst out laughing. "Me? Adorable?"

"Well, yeah, you're like a scary stuffed animal—cuddly but ferocious."

"Do you prefer me cuddly or ferocious?" he asked, moving closer to me.

I swallowed hard and tried to remember how to breathe as I stared at his shirtless perfection. "You are really … hot, Oswin. It's hard to think clearly when you're near me."

His mouth was on mine a millisecond later. I didn't deny him. Hell, I couldn't deny him. The all-consuming fear I'd had a minute ago was now a fading memory. He made sure of that. He devoured the hesitance and worry I'd felt before with every sweep of his lips against mine. There was nothing but him, nothing but the heat of his skin and the feel of his hands on my body.

Oswin pulled away and took my purse from my hands, tossing it on the foot of the bed. "Maybe an overnight stay was a bad idea," he said. "It's kind of the opposite of taking it slow."

I pouted. "So, no sex?"

Springing up from the bed with a playful grin, he held out his hand to me. "Oh, there will be sex. I just need to eat first. I've got a werewolf metabolism, you know."

I accepted his help then slid my hands up his arms to his biceps. "You've got a lot of werewolfy things," I purred. "I'm glad I came tonight."

Taking a firm hold on my waist, he looked me in the eye and spoke in a low, heated voice. "You're welcome to come anytime you like, Korrina."

Heat bloomed throughout me. "You keep saying nice things like that, and we'll never make it to dinner."

He shrugged and cupped my ass. "Works for me. We can get it delivered. Now take off your clothes. You need to get to my level of nakedness."

So much for taking things slow. The whole idea was absurd, anyway. When two highly sexual, reasonably attractive creatures were put together, sex was inevitable. I glanced down to the tent in his towel. Like, really inevitable.

I wrenched my sweater off and quickly cast it aside, not wanting to lose my nerve and ruin what was about to happen. That turned out to be an unnecessary worry. Just when I expected to have his undivided attention on my bare chest, Oswin backed away from me and picked up his cell phone. "What do you want on your pizza?"

I covered my naked breasts with an arm. "Whatever you're having is fine."

Speaking quickly into the phone, he set it down on the dresser and turned to me with a questioning look. "Why are you covering yourself?"

"I didn't feel I had your full attention," I said, just a tiny bit sourly.

His eyes twinkled. He was trying not to laugh. "Korrina, I haven't eaten since six this morning. If I'm going to be able to do what I plan on doing to you, I'm going to need food ... and so are you." He tugged the towel from his hips and threw it in the general direction of the bathroom. "Also," He motioned to his erection. "Never doubt that you have my full attention. I'm a hunter. I miss nothing. Now please take off your clothes, as I asked."

I had definite mixed emotions about Oswin's demanding personality. While it was a complete turn on to have him tell me what he wanted, it also scared me a little. Wolves were so naturally dominant—especially the Alphas. I didn't want him to feel like he could control me. "You miss nothing, huh? Okay, if that is true, what am I thinking right now?"

His sexy smile told me he knew everything. Pulling me closer, he started unzipping my skirt, never taking his eyes from my face. "I have no idea what you're thinking. Would you like to know what I'm thinking?"

Eyes wide, I nodded and held my breath.

"All right, I am thinking that despite the courage you work so hard to portray, you still fear me ... and my wolf. I also think that you hunger for me. These scents are like a punch to my system, and both of them make me hard for you."

Going down on one knee, he slowly peeled my panties down to my ankles, and I stepped out of them. His lingering hot breath on my thighs made me exhale in a shudder. I desperately wanted him to touch me, taste me, fuck me—whatever he was willing to do to me.

He stood and admired what he'd uncovered. "I think you are beautiful, Korrina. Just looking at you makes me ache to be inside of you."

I tensed. His voice was harsh, a hoarse, gravelly sound. His wolf was close to the surface.

"But I also think you fucked Obsidian," he continued. "No, I know you fucked him."

Shame racked me. "I'm sorry that I didn't tell you," I told him in a quiet voice. "I didn't want to hurt your feelings."

He stroked my cheek, his anger barely contained. "I thought with him losing his wife, he'd leave you alone. I see now how foolish that thought was. Hell, look at you. Who wouldn't want to fuck you?"

His face was nothing short of livid, and I knew this would be the end between us if I didn't do something about it. "Don't let my mistake come between us!" I blurted out hopelessly, not able to decide whether I really wanted him to give me a second chance or if I wanted him to send me away so I could crawl back to Obsidian and beg him to forgive me for coming here tonight. I wasn't sure what the right path was, just that I wanted them both.

Oswin cupped my face in his hands, running his thumb over my lip before kissing it lightly, almost curtly. "I do forgive you, darlin', but I'm also very, very angry. I'm angry that you let him taste you, that you took him inside of you, and that you chose him over me."

"It was a horrible lapse of judgment," I said sultrily. Who knew fear could be such a turn on? I was terrified of him, of what he might do, but shamelessly aroused. "It won't happen again."

Turning me around to face the bed, he spoke softly against my ear. "That it was, and it's one you're going to be punished for."

"Punished?" My voice wavered, the lust in it unmistakable.

"Yes. I'm going to punish you for lying to me … and for wanting him, of course." He growled low. "Close your eyes, nymph."

I did what he asked of me, though I wasn't sure how long my shaking legs would hold my weight up in the heels I was wearing. "What are you going to do?"

I could feel his hot breath on my neck as he pressed his hardness into the small of my back. "Rest assured, Korrina. You will survive tonight, and you will come back for more."

"Bold words," I told him, laughing at his arrogance. "You sound very sure of yourself."

"Do you doubt what I'm capable of, nymph?" he asked, his voice barely above a whisper.

"I—" I started, then I stopped, afraid to say anything else.

"Good girl," he said approvingly.

I gasped and tumbled face first onto the bed when he pushed me off balance. Glaring at him, I moved to stand up.

"Stay as you are!" he commanded, kneeling on the bed beside me. He smoothed his hand along the curve of my bottom. "You have no idea how appealing you are in this position. I can't decide whether I want to spank your ass red or fuck you until you can't walk out of here. What do you think I should do, darlin'?"

Before I could answer, he swung. I yelped out a surprised cry at the first stinging slap and tried to take each repetition in silence. Soon, that became impossible. His pace grew faster, harder until I couldn't hold back the tears or my cries of pain mixed with exquisite pleasure. He wasn't hitting hard enough to cause a welt, but I would have the imprints of his hand on me for several hours. "Please, Oswin," I begged him, beyond ready to feel him inside of me.

"Tell me what you want," he said, trailing the barest hint of claw across the skin he'd made sore and sensitive.

"I want you to fuck me," I panted, arching myself into his hand.

He slid his other hand down to cup the heated flesh between my thighs, making me gasp. "You're so wet, Korrina. Did the vampire make you this wet?"

I froze, the answer stuck on the tip of my tongue. I might have been near blind with desire, but I wasn't a fool. Oswin was an Alpha wolf, one that I didn't know all that well. Telling him I had thoroughly enjoyed sex with his enemy could be suicide.

"Don't be afraid," he whispered. "I'm not going to hurt you. I just want to know how Obsidian Raines managed to steal my female." Sliding two fingers inside me, he chuckled at the little surprised squeak I made. "Did he touch you like this?"

"Yes!" I cried out, my back bowing when he thumbed my clit.

He pushed his erection against my hip and shifted his weight. "Did he make you come?" When I didn't answer right away, he pushed his fingers deep and growled, "Korrina, I want to know."

I gasped. "Yes, many times."

"And did he?" he asked, his thumb circling at a maddeningly steady pace.

"Yes," I told him, looking back to meet his gaze. "Until it spilled down my thighs."

His body seem to jerk involuntarily before his irises burned with the bright yellow of his wolf. With a mouth full of sharpened teeth, he growled, "It's a very good thing I'm in control of my wolf. He aches to force you to be his submissive."

My hands gripping his comforter and my toes curled tight, I threw my head back as I writhed against his hand. "How would he accomplish that, Oswin?"

He kept his voice low, his tone menacing. "The same way I plan to. He would claim you as his mate."

We stilled at the same time. Him, because he heard something in the front yard. Me, because his words terrified me. He apologetically slid his fingers from me and jumped to his feet seconds before the doorbell rang.

"We're not done here," he said. "Don't move a muscle."

I didn't dare. I only watched him with my tearstained cheeks burning from embarrassment and the most hardcore sexual experience of my life. He gave me a wink as he put on his jeans then walked into the kitchen, closing the door behind him.

"Korrina?" a confused voice asked.

I scrambled around to see Obsidian materialize behind me. "What are you doing here?" I whispered, mortified beyond belief.

"That's the Bureau at the door. They know you left town without permission. Put your arms around me; I can mist you out of here. We'll try to convince the officers that you've been at my place the whole time. It's all we can do."

Scared out of my mind, I jumped up and looked wildly around me. "Where's my purse?"

He pointed to the end of the bed and quickly grabbed my skirt, bra, panties, and sweater from the floor. "I've got your clothes."

I hurried into Obsidian's arms, and we evaporated into nothing.

CAUGHT BETWEEN A ROCK AND A HARD COCK

OBSIDIAN

We were a good sixty miles away from the pack site when I finally felt we were safe enough to materialize. All of the Bureau's cars that had been at Oswin's had passed us as we hid in the fog on the side of the road, and thankfully, the pack master hadn't sent any wolves to track us.

Korrina was shivering from the cold, or maybe, from fear as she walked. I honestly didn't care which. Incensed, enraged, furious… not one of those words could accurately describe how I felt about Korrina's betrayal. I ask her to be my bride, and instead, she chooses to have sex games with my sworn enemy? What. The. Fuck?

"Get dressed," I told her, callously thrusting her clothes into her hands and none too gently ushering her toward the tree line. I needed her clothed, now. Seeing her naked with Oswin made me want to redden her ass myself vehemently.

"O-okay," she said, between chattering teeth, tears starting to slip down her cheeks.

I looked to the heavens. How did she always manage to make me feel remorse? Sighing, I put an arm around her and pulled her to my side. "Don't cry, love. We'll get past this. You'll see."

"I don't deserve your pity," she sobbed. "You were right. I am a whore."

"No, you're not. I should have never said that to you."

Korrina pointed out her obvious nudity. "Obsidian, you asked me to marry you, and I went out and tried to fuck the first dick I could find, just like you said I would. That's not normal behavior."

"Are you kidding me?" I asked. "You're a nymph, Korrina.

93

It's not that surprising sex is your crutch when you're upset."

"Maybe not," she said, fresh tears coming to her eyes. "But I'm going to go to jail for this. I knew better than to leave town. Why did I even do it? I could've just slept with you if I wanted sex that bad."

"I suspect that this was more of an attempt to make me jealous and show me what I keep trying to push away than the actions of a wanton woman," I told her.

She sniffled. "I think that's exactly what I was doing ... at first."

That pause told me I was going to hate what I was about to hear. "And then?"

"I liked what he did to me," she said, eyes gleaming with a mixture of tears and uncontrolled lust. "I liked him punishing me for choosing you."

The instant I heard her words, my dick got hard. I liked watching her take his wrath. It was surprisingly satisfying. I leaned in close. "As much as I hated seeing Oswin with his hands on you, watching you take his punishment for fucking me will keep me hard for the next century."

She was stricken, mortified. I knew she would be. "You saw it?"

I smiled wickedly. "Every single second of it. Was sex with me worth it?"

"Oh, yes, Obsidian. It was so worth it." She glanced around us, suddenly distracted.

On the alert, I glanced in the direction she'd looked, sending my senses outward. I didn't pick up anything. "What is it, Korrina?"

She didn't say anything. She just attacked, pressing her naked body against me and kissing me like it would be the last kiss of her life. Easing her off, I spun her around to the tree behind her. She leaned against it and looked back seductively. "Obsidian?"

"Just give me one second to appreciate the sight of you against that tree," I said. "Then I'm going to fuck you in a way that would make the wolf use more than his hand to punish you." I unzipped my pants and palmed my throbbing shaft. "Are you ready for me, Korrina?"

She whimpered in the affirmative. Not that it mattered. I would be inside of her in three seconds. Wrapping her long hair around my fist, I pulled her head back as I pushed deep into her. She was hungry for me, setting the rhythm at a pace I would have thought only a vampire capable of. "Is this what you were thinking about when the wolf was punishing you?" I asked, nipping at her shoulder. "Or was it my bite?"

I bit into her again, not caring if I hurt her or even waiting for her to answer. When she screamed out in orgasm, I let my hunger take over and bit her again—and again—and again.

***

Korrina was serene by the time we made it to Goshen. She seemed to have accepted her fate the only way she could—by quietly fretting on the inside. Her eyes held some of the fear she was trying to ignore, but her body was still, sitting stiffly on the sofa in the parlor in wait.

"You'll have to water the bougainvillea plants in the back," she said suddenly. "They need a little extra care after my meltdown. And don't forget to speak to the trees occasionally. They seem to be coming around to you."

I sat next to her on the sofa and let her wrap her arms around me. She laid a cheek on the place my heartbeat would've been. "You can't hear it, I told her. "But it beats for you."

Her shoulders shook with repressed tears. "I keep messing things up. Why can't I seem to do the right thing?"

I tipped her face up to mine and kissed her wet cheeks. "You haven't done anything wrong. There's no mess where we're

95

concerned."

"Promise?" she asked, her voice small.

I gently pressed her head into my chest, squeezing my eyes shut tight. "I promise, Korrina. I will make this right."

Only an hour later, I watched the Bureau officers put Korrina into the backseat of their car. I had never hated myself more. I was embarrassed by the way I'd treated her. I cringed at the memory of every insult. But I was most ashamed of taking advantage of her in the woods. In her emotional state, she'd been brutally honest with me, and I'd repaid that honesty by marking her until she cried out with more pain than pleasure. And I'd done it right after I called Solon with her whereabouts in Thomasville.

What a fucking mistake that had been. Uncle or not, he was a stickler for the law. I knew that. Of course, I knew that. But the petty, territorial lover in me had wanted to teach her a lesson for her unfaithfulness, wanted to punish her just like Oswin had. Now, I wanted to gouge out my eyes so I couldn't see her cry, alone and handcuffed in the back of a patrol car.

As I watched the car's red tail lights fade into the night, I felt something snap inside of me. Rushing to the bedroom, I grabbed a pair of running shoes and jammed my feet into them. I launched myself out the door and ran down the road as fast as I could in a half-mist state. My future wife couldn't … wouldn't go to prison. Not now, not ever.

**

Forty-five minutes later, I came to a skidding stop in the parking lot of the Bureau's small transfer station in Greenville. Unsurprisingly, Solon was waiting for me at a side entrance.

"You know I had to do it," he said, walking down the steps to greet me. "She broke the law."

"I understand the law, Solon. And I understand your need to uphold it. After eighty years, I ought to. But surely you can forgive

Korrina of this. It is such a small infraction."

He put a hand on my shoulder. "I can't stop the arrest. It's out of my hands. She knew I couldn't help her outside of Meadowbrook."

I nodded and sighed. "Will she go to the Bureau's prison?"

"Of course not. She will be booked here to await punishment. As you said, it is a small infraction."

I sent a thankful look up to the heavens. At least, one thing would go right tonight. "Good. What will her punishment be?"

Solon pursed his lips. "I'm thinking of confining her to house arrest in a heavily supervised halfway house."

Hope blossomed in my chest. If I could somehow convince Solon to let me host Korrina at my house, it could put an end to the mess I'd caused and ensure that Korrina wouldn't be able to risk her safety with Oswin again.

"May I suggest my own home instead of the halfway house? I can supervise her at any hour. You know I don't have to sleep."

Solon's face was the picture of suspicion. "That would be a preferable outcome," he said carefully. "But why would you offer her this?"

I leveled my stare on him. "I love her. I have asked her to be my bride."

"Indeed? And has she accepted?"

"No, but I expect her to."

"Even after she has been caught at another male's house?"

I chuckled. It was typical of him to go right for the throat. "She has only been with me, before and after her trip out of town."

"Even so, I'm going to give you a moment to think this through, Obsidian. She will be informed that it was you that called attention to her whereabouts tonight. Don't expect her to be happy about that."

"I don't. In fact, I expect her to be furious. I will weather it. It's best if we don't have secrets between us."

"You are a male of worth," Solon said, shaking my hand.

I sighed. "I've been such an idiot since she showed up at the house. She makes me crazy, Solon."

He clasped his hands behind his back and nodded toward the end of the building where I could hear the officers unloading Korrina from their car. "Sounds like love to me."

I followed him to the back, continuing my self-deprecating diatribe in a whisper. "I wasn't thinking when I called you. I just couldn't stand the thought of her being with Oswin."

His dark brows winged up. "Oswin? Oswin Morris?"

I nodded. "The one and only."

"Then you were right to call me. Now that I know who she was spending time with, I'm grateful you did. We all know Oswin to be an unsavory fellow with a penchant for murdering those who oppose him. I don't know if I could rest if I knew she was to become his Alpha female."

"I know exactly how you feel," I muttered.

He clapped me on the shoulder. "Come on, old friend. I'll take you to her."

***

Korrina's relief was palpable when she saw us enter the room outside her cell ten minutes later. "Uncle, Obsidian, what's going to happen to me?"

Solon smiled and unlocked the cell door. "Obsidian is going to take you to his home. He will be your guardian until your first punishment in Goshen is complete. Consider yourself on house arrest."

"Thank you, Uncle." She turned her alleviated smile on me. "Thanks for coming so fast."

Her grateful expression made me feel like the shmuck I was. I didn't deserve her admiration after what I'd done. "Korrina, don't thank me just yet. You will soon be very angry with me."

Realization and hurt were plain on her face. "You called them. How could you, Obsidian?"

I stepped closer, but she backed away. Ignoring the movement, I said, "I'm not going to lie to you. I called Solon when I learned you didn't heed my warning about the wolves. I panicked, Korrina. I wouldn't have done it if I didn't love you and care about your safety."

She closed the cell door between us, unmoved by my admission. "No, Uncle, I will not submit to this."

Solon's expression hardened as he stared his niece down. "Korrina, you broke the law. You don't have the right to demand anything. You will accompany Mr. Raines to his home and move your things into his house. And you will be civil to him. He is the only reason you aren't sharing a house with twenty career prostitutes right now. You should be thanking him, not condemning him for caring about your welfare."

Korrina scoffed. "Not fucking likely."

"Watch your mouth, young lady!" Solon warned her, then he winked at me. "Obsidian, as her ward, I need you to sign some papers, then you can take her home. I'll have someone bring your car from my house to the jail."

"Sounds good," I replied, appalled by his humorous take on the situation but delighted by my good fortune.

Solon stopped in front of Korrina, clearly trying to express unspoken words to her with his eyes. "This is your last chance, youngling," he said finally. "Don't screw it up."

Korrina wouldn't look at him, but she muttered, "Yes, sir."

***

Three hours later, the car had been delivered, the papers had been signed, and we were on our way home. As expected, Korrina glared at me with an icy stare the first few minutes of the drive. After that, she resorted to trying to upset me with her words.

"I hope you don't think I'll ever marry you now," she said. "You betrayed me."

"I think your definition of betrayed is slightly skewed," I told her. "I wasn't being disloyal to our friendship or our relationship. I was out of my mind with worry for the safety of the female I might call my wife. There's nothing wrong with that."

She screamed under her breath in frustration. "Nothing wrong? I was arrested tonight!"

I nodded, trying to appease her. "Yes, but you knew that was a possibility when you left your house, didn't you? That's what you told me after I took you from Oswin's."

"Of course, I did, psycho," she huffed.

"Look, I understand that you are going to be mad for a while, but please understand, I did what I did out of love. I love you, Korrina."

She gave me a deadpan look. "Fuck you and your love, Obsidian. If I weren't being subjected to the torture of living with you, I would never see you again."

INSANITY - POPULATION 1

KORRINA

October 17th

   I will not stake Obsidian.

   I will not stake Obsidian.

   I will not stake Obsidian.

   Oh, fuck it.

K

"I hate your stupid, handsome face," I said for the hundredth time since we'd left Meadowbrook. I mean, I didn't say it out loud or anything, but boy, was I thinking it. I refused to go down without a fight. Obsidian owed me an apology. A big one.

"What are you thinking?" Obsidian asked, giving me the side-eye.

He was obviously trying to gauge my feelings. He'd periodically asked inane questions the entire trip. The jackass. "I'm wondering if vampire's dicks grow back if they're severed off," I answered sweetly.

He winced. "Korrina, really."

"Just stop trying to talk to me," I muttered, staring straight ahead.

"As you wish," he conceded. "For now."

I spent the afternoon moving my things into Obsidian's house—all while studiously ignoring his every offer of pleasantry and help. It was so damn hard. According to the papers I signed at the jail, I wasn't allowed to drive my car. At the time, I didn't think it was that big of a deal. Now I understood the errors of my naive thoughts. After the third trip next door, I started to realize the number of books in my collection was borderline ridiculous and had a hard time convincing myself that that was just the moving madness talking.

By dusk, the last of my things were packed into their boxes, and it was way past time for a break. Stretching my back, I poured a glass of tea and walked out onto the porch. The only sounds were crickets and the wind blowing through the trees. I smiled. It was really nice out here, living so far away from civilization. No horns honking or dogs barking, no noisy neighbors, just sweet, peaceful solitude and the smell of honeysuckle.

Setting my glass on the railing, I sat in the rocker and propped up my tired feet, staring down the darkened driveway, not really seeing anything until I noticed a faint glowing in the distance. Unsure of what I was seeing, I rubbed my eyes. It was still there. Planting my feet on the porch, I eased up from the chair and sprinted to the edge of the yard, hiding behind a pine tree. From there, I could see the ghostly outline of a young woman sauntering in my direction, the full moon illuminating her white nightgown. What was she doing down here at this time of night?

"Hi," I called out. "Can I help you with something?"

The woman turned to me with glazed, unseeing eyes, unperturbed by the interruption. Without slowing her cadence, she continued her march up the road toward Obsidian's house without a word.

Suspicion ignited in me. This woman wasn't some ghostly apparition. This was a woman being called to slaughter. And Obsidian was the only one around here who could be the butcher.

Clinching my fists in anger, I trailed behind the girl, staying out of sight. It didn't take long to hear Obsidian's soft-spoken voice beckoning to her, coaxing her to him. I was right. She was Obsidian's supper tonight.

On hands and knees, I crept closer to the sound of his voice until I could see Obsidian's bare moonlit shoulders in the distance. Flushing with heat, I couldn't help but admire how beautifully built he was and how strong the arms holding the hypnotized woman to his chest were. She didn't seem to mind being there, either. The throaty, almost sexual sigh urging him on made that clear. I couldn't blame her. At that moment, I wasn't angry at what he was doing; I craved to be in her position.

I was on the verge of yelling for him to stop, to tell him to take me instead when he lunged and bit savagely into her neck. Stifling a scream, I turned and crept away, scrambling as fast as I could through the brush. Once on my feet, I didn't stop running until I made it into my old house and had locked the doors behind me.

No more than two minutes later, a pounding on the door startled a scream out of me.

"Korrina, open the door."

It sounded like Obsidian, but his voice was off, almost crazed. I moved to the space between the door and the window and leaned my back against the wood. "Sure, I'll just skip right over and forget you just took advantage of a girl who barely looked old enough to vote."

"I can smell your hunger from here. You want me. Open the door."

"Everything isn't about sex, Obsidian. Besides, you have that human woman out there. What do you need me for?"

"She's food, Korrina. I don't fuck unwilling women."

"You just eat them? That's so much better," I said sarcastically.

"You don't know she is unwilling in that capacity. This is ridiculous. Open the door."

I was tempted—so tempted.

"You have to come out sometime," he taunted. "You're confined to my house, remember."

"I'll come out when it's daylight," I countered.

His enraged growl vibrated the wall. "I can come in there anytime I want. It's my house."

He had me there. He probably had a key in his pocket right now. "Do you promise not to hurt me if I open the door?" The sex we'd last had was probably the best I'd ever experienced, but it had been borderline painful.

There was a lengthy pause. "No."

That word undid me. I flipped the lock on the door and waited, holding my breath. Nothing happened. He didn't open the door or say anything else. After a minute, I turned the knob myself and swung the door wide, quickly returning to the safety of the wall. Nothing. Finally summoning the courage to look outside, I peeked out the doorway. He was gone. I sighed in relief, or maybe, disappointment and stepped out onto the porch to retrieve the tea glass.

Obsidian's mocking laugh sounded behind me. "Now that I have the advantage, I wonder if you will run."

I froze with my back to him. I could run, but I knew I'd never make it to the trees before he caught me. "I'm not going to run," I told him.

"Such bravery," he said, his breath tickling my ear.

"What do you want?" I asked in a whisper, my breath coming in shallow gasps.

"You know what I want."

"No, I don't."

He spun me around to face him, his amber eyes now an angry black. "Why do you torment me? You know I'd never touch another female. I asked you to be my bride, Korrina!"

"Then why did you call that woman tonight?" I asked, my tone frosty.

"I told you. She is a means of sustenance. I have to feed, or I will die."

I gave him a vicious smile. "And wouldn't that just be too bad?"

He returned my sardonic smile with interest, fangs at the ready. "Korrina, I know you love the prospect of getting rid of me altogether. However, you shouldn't forget. Without me, you'll go to a group home for the next five years. I'm sure even you can't prefer that to a soft bed, a hard dick, and someone who loves you."

I threw my hands up. "You're right, Obsidian. You're absolutely right. I don't want to go to prison. And I do want you."

"Are you saying that you love me?" he asked, gripping my arms.

"Yes," I answered tentatively, worried that he would misconstrue my words before I could finish them. "I just can't trust you."

His expression made me jerk my arms from his grip and take a step back.

"Why are you so fucking infuriating?" he snarled, cornering me against the railing.

"I don't know!" I yelled, before ducking around him to run into the house and slamming the door in his face … and then opening it, marching past him to grab the tea glass I left and storming back in.

I heard Obsidian laugh. "So, I'll see you at home?"

PAYBACK HURTS ... A LOT
OBSIDIAN

I woke the next morning to blinding light and searing pain. The sun was a pinkish glow on the horizon, but it burned me like a hot iron. Roaring in agony, I leaped out of bed and sped to the safety and darkness of the hallway. What had happened to my blackout drapes?

"Missing something?" Korrina asked. She was standing across from the doorway with the drapes folded neatly in a laundry basket.

Was she fucking serious? "You could have killed me, Korrina!" I yelled, pointing to my singed arm for emphasis.

She narrowed her eyes. "Yeah, and you could have sent me to the Bureau's prison indefinitely if my uncle didn't intervene. I'd say we're even."

Throwing the basket at my feet, she stomped into the living room and turned on the television. Me? I hurriedly retreated to my office, locked the door, and propped a chair under the knob for good measure. I wasn't taking any chances with Korrina today. I knew I drove her crazy, but I didn't think we'd ever get to the level where homicide seemed like the appropriate response to ... well, anything.

I collapsed on the sofa, making sure to land as far from the window as I could. It was heavily draped, but I'd been burned twice this week. A 'third time's a charm' scenario wasn't something I was willing to risk.

***

Still wary of what was to come, I didn't leave my office until after two in the morning. I wouldn't have left at all if my healing hadn't taken most of the energy from my last feeding. I needed to feed tonight, or I'd be in serious pain tomorrow. There was a second where I briefly entertained the idea of asking Korrina for her blood. However, that thought was quickly squelched by the notion she would probably stake me in my sleep if I did that right now. She was a wildcard. I couldn't be sure what she would do next.

Tentatively, I walked down the hallway and glanced in at Korrina. She was cocooned on the couch in a fuzzy blanket, watching Wuthering Heights.

"Hi," she said in a small voice.

I fought the ridiculous urge to arm myself and entered the room. "Good evening, Korrina. I hope you are well."

"I'm surprised to hear you say that," she said, her voice muffled by the blanket. "I thought you'd still be angry."

I sighed. "I am … disturbed. You knew you would injure me, did you not?"

"Yes," she replied meekly. Sitting up, she gestured to the cushion next to her. "Can you sit for a minute?"

"I'm sorry, no. I have to feed now if I'm going to tonight. It's almost half past two."

Inexplicably, she became more fragile before my eyes. "You're feeding from someone else?"

I took her hand in mine and dared to press my lips to her palm. "Korrina, you tried to burn me alive less than a day ago. I didn't think feeding me would be on the top of your to-do list."

Tears appeared in her eyes. "This is bullshit."

I frowned, not understanding what she meant. "I'm sorry?"

"You promised you would spend time with me in exchange for my blood before I even moved in here. You've never once made good on that promise."

I had no argument. Her righteous anger was wholly justified. She was right. I had days to make good on my promise and didn't.

Was it possible that she could set me on fire and still be a better person than me? Fuck.

"You're right, Korrina. I'm sorry. And I promise I will make it up to you."

She raised an eyebrow. "How?"

That was an excellent question. One I didn't have an answer for. "You let me worry about that," I hedged. "You let me worry about everything."

I received a tight hug for taking a step we both knew I should have taken long ago. I had a hard time letting go. My fangs sprang into my mouth the moment her scent hit me. She smelled so good, so warm and familiar, I couldn't help but want her.

Korrina smiled wearily and shoved her wrist at me as she pulled out of our embrace. "You're hungry, Obsidian. Eat."

Nodding, I slipped an arm around her waist and bit into the tender skin of her neck. The blood flowed fast and warm into my mouth. I moaned at the electric current on my tongue.

"I'm glad you came out of your office while I was awake," she said, absently running her fingers through my hair. Knowing I couldn't converse with her had never seemed to dissuade her from having a conversation with me while I fed.

"Me, too," I murmured before closing her wounds and licking my lips to savor the flavor. Korrina's blood was full of life, and magic, and wild energy that made me feel more alive than I'd felt since I was a young vampire. It intoxicated me.

She sighed. "I wanted to apologize right away, but I just couldn't. My pride, it wouldn't let me. Do you ever think we both have too much pride?"

"Every single day, love." I kissed the healing bite. "Korrina, I forgive you for what you did … for all of what you did. They were such little things compared to what I've done. I've been such an ass to you."

"You said it, not me." She grinned at the sour face I gave her and stood up, stretching her arms above her head.

I caught her hand as she lowered it. "And I meant it."

"Good," she said, yawning. "I'm really sleepy. Care to cuddle with me for a little while?"

"Cuddle?" I asked.

She smirked, giving me a knowing look. "Yeah, cuddling. You spoon me and keep your penis to yourself."

I laughed. When she and I were on speaking terms, we could barely be in the same room without having sex. A plan to cuddle had no hope of success.

"What's so funny?" she asked, eyeing me speculatively.

"It's nothing." Still smiling, I scooped her up and carried her to her bedroom.

She looked confused when we arrived at her door. "Why are we going to my bedroom?"

I gave her a light squeeze. "Because my room doesn't have curtains, remember?"

Her cheeks blushed pink. "Yes, it does. I hung them back up this morning."

"Everything is forgiven," I told her, kissing her furrowed forehead. "Don't even think about it. I want a clean slate between us."

She smiled up at me. "I'm really glad."

That made two of us.

Once in the bedroom, I laid Korrina on my bed and watched her wriggle under the blankets to pull them up to her chin. I sat next to her, and she closed her eyes, letting out a little sigh.

"The covers smell like you," she said.

Grinning, I knelt, busying myself with stacking wood and

lighting the fireplace as I listened to her make happy, sleepy noises. Even after everything that had happened between us, she still liked the way I smelled. I was glad she couldn't see my goofy smile.

VAMPIRES ARE HOPELESSLY CONFUSING
KORRINA

October 22nd

Nothing Obsidian does surprises me anymore. Nothing. Once you learn to expect the unexpected, it all just seems like a walk in the park. And I have to admit, I kind of like it. It certainly keeps my interest piqued anyway. Not that it wasn't already. We are talking about Obsidian 'ridiculously sexy vampire' Raines, are we not?

K

The more time I spent with Obsidian, the more I noticed how strange he was. On the surface, he seemed normal, living every day almost as a human would. He cleaned, paid bills online, did yard work, and occasionally watched TV with me. But, at times, I saw the real vampire he kept hidden, and it unnerved me.

I told myself he was getting used to me being around, he was showing me his true face, but I didn't really believe that. What I believed was the truth. Obsidian wasn't human. And while he was a master at putting on an illusion, he couldn't keep it up all the time.

The first night I saw his human façade slip, he was reading in his library. I was doing my usual, flitting about the room, searching for the perfect book and not paying much attention to him, when I heard a low growl. I froze in place, covertly glancing in my periphery. There Obsidian sat, the book he'd been reading open in his lap. He was unnaturally still as he stared at me, his eyes as black as coal. He was every bit the predator humans and supernaturals feared.

Heart racing, I dropped the book I was holding. His eyes

darted to the book then back to me. "Try to be more careful, Korrina," he said, picking up the forgotten book in his lap. "That book is older than both of us combined."

"S-sorry," I stammered, bewildered by what had just happened.

In a split-second, Obsidian had gone from cold-blooded killer to his usual waspish persona. It should have given me relief, but it had the opposite effect. It scared me. And totally turned me on. I might have to lock myself in my room and sleep with the light on tonight, but I'd be thinking about how hot he looked as he stared at me with hunger like I'd never seen on any male before.

***

A week into my house arrest, Obsidian finally made his first move and asked me to keep him company while he watched TV. We'd progressed to a constant state of flirtation, but we weren't doing much else, much to my dismay, so I took the invitation as a really good sign.

I'd managed to talk him into watching a movie of my choice, a minor miracle. Obsidian was notoriously picky about his entertainment. I chose my old copy of Vénus beauté (institut) because … sex. I wanted it, badly. And this movie had some of the most intense sex scenes in cinematic history. If there was anything left in this world that was good and decent, this movie would get me laid.

Halfway through the movie, I poked him with a toe and smirked at his rapt face. "I thought you said you didn't like this movie."

He didn't take his eyes from the screen. "It does have its attributes."

"You said it was utter tripe and practically porn forty-five minutes ago," I teased, walking my fingers up his knee.

He weakly swatted my hand away but didn't glance away from the movie. I knew why. The cries of pleasure echoing from the speakers told me exactly which part of the film he was so enthralled with. Two lovers would be passionately making love against a wall. It was hot and animalistic and one of the sexiest scenes I'd ever witnessed.

Ah, dirty French movies. Is there anything better on Earth?

Nope.

Obsidian licked his lips. "Utter tripe? I don't recall ever saying that in my life."

I tugged on the blanket covering us both. "You're a liar and a blanket stealer!"

In a low voice, he asked, "Would you rather me expose you to my hard dick or steal the blanket? You'll have to pick one."

I yanked the blanket off his lap. "I choose to be exposed."

His eyes flashed to mine then shot to the door. "You don't want to do that, Korrina."

I cocked my head, looking longingly at his lap. "Yes. Yes, I do."

He cupped my jaw, stroking my cheek with his thumb. "I really hate to disappoint you."

"That will never happen," I purred, giving him a naughty smile and climbing into his lap. I nipped my way up the line of his neck. "You've never disappointed me before."

He groaned and stood with me latched on to him, staring intently at the door. "And hopefully, this will be the only time."

Pouting prettily, I crossed my arms in front of me. "I hope there's a good reason."

Setting me on my feet, he whispered, "There is. Your uncle is here."

"Oh, shit!" I hissed, frantically looking for the remote. My uncle finding out his best friend was watching softcore porn with his niece was something I desperately wanted to avoid. Spying it

114

on the floor, I fumbled the remote a couple times before I managed to turn the TV off.

Obsidian glanced down at me when the doorbell rang. "Think this is bad news?"

"Only one way to find out." Taking a deep breath, I squared my shoulders and walked to the door, swinging it wide. Solon stood there, wearing his usual grey suit and a broad grin. I rushed out to hug him. "Uncle, Solon!"

He picked me up and swung me around, a greeting as natural to us as breathing. "There's my baby girl!"

"Come in!" I exclaimed, grabbing his hand when he put me on my feet. "What are you doing here?"

Solon let me drag him in, laughing at my enthusiasm. "Obsidian, is she always like this when guests come over?"

"I don't entertain guests, as you well know," Obsidian answered, stepping forward to shake his friend's hand. "But yes, Korrina is … a force of nature."

I smacked his arm. "I'm going to take that as a compliment."

Obsidian wrapped an arm around me and kissed the top of my head. "You should."

The smile on Solon's face was nearly Grinch-like in its smugness. "I see you two are getting along nicely."

I narrowed my eyes. "Yes, and who could have foreseen that?"

He chuckled. "Well, sometimes, fate needs a shove or two."

"In our case, it might have to be ten," I told him, smacking Obsidian again when he gave me a tight squeeze. "You know I'm right, Obsidian. We've sucked at our relationship so far."

Solon snickered. "I hear it gets easier over time. And as luck would have it, you have about fifty-nine months to become familiar with each other."

"I want to spend an eternity becoming familiar with Korrina," Obsidian told him, smiling down at me. "If only someone would accept my ring."

Feigning exasperation, I threw my hands up. "I'm going to. Just give me ten seconds to get out of jail and pull my shit together, okay?"

He wrapped me in his strong arms, and for a moment, I could imagine a pulse that beat in unison with my own heart. "I will wait forever if that's what it takes," he whispered.

I lifted my eyes to his. There was so much warmth and sincerity in them, I could hardly get the words I wanted to say out of my mouth. "I—I'll marry you, Obsidian."

With intensity practically radiating from his entire body, he cupped my face. "Don't toy with me, Korrina."

I grinned. "Well, where's the fun in that?"

"Korrina," Obsidian warned.

"Obsidian," I deadpanned.

Solon cleared his throat. "Should I leave you two alone?"

Obsidian shook his head. "Of course not. As a matter of fact, I think it's about time you tell us why you're really here." He turned back to me. "We will continue this."

"You know where I live," I said brightly.

"Such sass," he said, shaking his head. "Solon, care to sit for a minute? I want to know what was so important you left Meadowbrook. You never leave Meadowbrook. You're a virtual recluse."

Solon inclined his head and laughed. "You were never one to mince words."

"Nor were you," Obsidian retorted. He sat in the wingback chair nearest to the fireplace, crooked his lips, and patted his lap. "Korrina?"

I found myself walking toward him without making the conscious decision to do so. It wasn't that I didn't want to come to him, I just didn't make the decision to do it. I lifted a brow at Obsidian. Did his mind control extend to nymphs?

Solon watched us get cozy with a self-satisfied smile stretched wide. "It seems your probationary period is going well."

"We got off to a bit of a bumpy start, but we seem to have worked it out," I told him, peering up at Obsidian for his confirmation.

Obsidian nodded in amused agreement. "I'd have to say, it's going better than expected."

"Good, good," Solon said, relaxing onto the couch. "That's nice to hear. But your welfare and adjustment to your new living arrangements aren't the only reasons I'm here."

Obsidian possessively clutched me to his body, as if he was afraid I'd get taken from his arms. "What is it, Solon?"

"It may be nothing, or it may be something," he said cryptically. "I thought it best to err on the side of caution with the information I got today."

"What information is that?" I asked.

He frowned. "The trees have reported that you have uninvited visitors around your house and property."

"I knew it!" Obsidian said triumphantly. "Since yesterday, I've smelled something out there. I just haven't been able to place the scent."

"That's because you've probably never met this particular creature. Satyrs tend to live near nymph communities, rarely traveling outside the immediate area."

"Why would a satyr come to my house? Does he sense Korrina here?"

Solon gave me the side eye. "This one has a history with my niece. I thought she might have told you about Agapios by now."

I tensed. After my breakdown, I told Obsidian I didn't want to talk about my convictions. It was too embarrassing for him to find out the truth. And the fact was, everyone knew nymphs that had sex with satyrs were past hope and mostly prostitutes. Nymphs always mated with other nymphs. They were fanatical about it. Only the most desperate of our race had sex with other supernaturals or humans. But me? I preferred sex with any other creature. I couldn't stand the nymphs that tried to court me into marriage. Big egos and mediocre skills in bed weren't exactly the things I was looking for in a lover or a long-term relationship. I needed more than that. I needed excitement and, ideally, multiple orgasms.

"We discussed my arrests, but not in detail," I explained. I found Obsidian's inquisitive gaze on me when I dared to glance up at his face. A warm, tingling sensation spread through me when our eyes met. He didn't look mad at all, just curious and a little devilish.

"What does Agapios want with Korrina?" he asked, never taking his eyes from mine.

Solon cleared his throat and lifted an eyebrow. "I can think of a few things. But it's not the satyr I'm worried about. Regardless of Agapios' … power of persuasion, I believe the Thomasville wolf pack poses a much more significant threat to you."

Obsidian straightened in his seat. "I haven't smelled any wolves in the area. Did the trees say how long this has been going on?"

"The first time was the day after Korrina's arrest. They've been careful to stay out of range, but the wolves are definitely up to something—something Oswin had no knowledge of when he called to offer diplomatic immunity to Korrina a week ago."

"Diplomatic immunity?" Obsidian asked. But that would mean…"

Solon cringed. "He would take her as his mate, yes. When I told him about the alternate punishment I'd chosen, he said he'd let things lie like they were, but he wanted Korrina to know the offer still stood if she wanted it. He's willing to wait as long as it takes."

"Oswin is not immortal," Obsidian fumed. "I am."

Solon held up his hands and said, "Don't shoot the messenger, old friend. I only wanted you to know what you have coming your way," then he tilted his head toward the door. "Can we speak in private for a few minutes, Korrina?"

My heart skipped a beat. Solon didn't do weird, clandestine meetings. That meant what he wanted to tell me was something about Obsidian, Oswin, or something so personal he didn't want my potential husband to overhear it.

I kissed Obsidian and stood. "Let me grab my coat."

Once outside, Solon quickly ushered me into his car and drove us to the driveway leading into Oswin's land.

"Do you think it's wise to trespass on an Alpha wolf's property right now?" I asked him. "The wolves could be out there."

He shook his head, but it was a minute or so before he gave me his attention. Silent conversation over, he muttered something under his breath then turned off the engine. "All right, youngling. I brought you out here for a multiple of reasons."

"I kind of figured that out, Solon. What the hell is going on?"

A furrow appeared between his black brows. "The trees are worried. They say the wolves keep referring to a plan."

"What kind of plan," I asked warily.

"The kind that gets you out of the picture. The Alphahood is serious business with the Thomasville pack, Korrina. Oswin's leadership is brand new. They know if they don't take control now, they'll never get it. I'm thinking they're banking on him having to forfeit the title because of his lack of mate. All they have to do is get rid of you somehow, and the pack is theirs."

I stared at him. "Are you serious?"

119

"I'm here, aren't I? Do you think I'd come all the way to Goshen to lie about something as important as this?"

"No," I muttered. "I'm sorry. I'm a little freaked out right now."

"That's completely understandable. But you might want to save your freak out until I tell you about Agapios."

I groaned. "What about Agapios?"

"He's currently M.I.A."

"And you think he's trying to find a place to hide out from the Bureau?" I couldn't think of another reason he'd come here, especially after the way he acted in court.

"I think he might mean to harm you."

Shocked, I asked, "Why?"

He sighed. "Korrina, Agapios was … well, I guess you could say 'displeased' with his punishment. In fact, he made a great spectacle in the courtroom when I read my verdict. It's all anyone has talked about since your departure."

"Glad to know I'm no longer the talk of the town," I groused. "But what does his punishment have to do with me?"

"He blames you, of course."

I sighed. "Of course he does. Has he given any indication as to why he blames me?"

"Not as of yet. But the moment we find out, I will tell you."

"Okay. Is there anything else while we're out here?"

"Yes."

I pouted. "Solon, I don't know how much more I can take."

He chuckled. "This isn't a bad thing. I just want to make sure you know what you're getting into with the vampire."

"You mean, the vampire that's an old friend of yours? The one you practically threw me at?"

"The very one," he said wryly. "Look, Korrina, I know you love each other. I can see it in the way you two communicate. There's a depth there I hadn't expected to see so fast."

"But?"

"But I want you to be sure this is really what you want to do. You are both immortal. This relationship will likely last an eternity. Are you sure you don't want to give it a little more thought before you jump in with both feet?"

I thought about it for a split-second. "I'm sure."

Solon pursed his lips. "You've known him for less than a month, Korrina. How can you be sure?"

"I just am," I said, shrugging. "I don't know what it is, but I think we're supposed to be together. It feels right. I trust him."

"Do you think it's wise to trust him?" he asked.

"You do."

"Yes, but I trust him because I've been his confidant since eighteen ninety-six. There's a fair bit of difference in our situations."

"In all that time, has he done anything to make you think he wouldn't be a good husband to me? I mean, you did trust him enough to send me here. I'm not seeing what the problem is."

"The problem is that he's acting in a way I'm unused to. I've never seen him so obsessed, even when he was married to Edith. Vampires, especially true vampires like Obsidian, don't do what he's doing."

"Says the guy acting totally out of character," I muttered.

He narrowed his eyes. "Korrina, he's acting on emotion. Vampires don't have emotions."

I laughed. "Every creature has emotions, Solon."

He shook his head. "If you would have met Obsidian before his marriage to Edith, you would not be saying that. He was a different male, cold and calculating, almost alien in the way he thought. He didn't care about love. Hell, I'm not entirely sure he cared about it when he was married. It's obvious he's changed. That's what concerns me."

"But that's good, right. Don't you want someone who cares about me for my mate?"

He laced his fingers with mine. "Of course I do. I just want to make sure you don't get hurt." He stared out the windshield, listening to the trees again before he continued. "In keeping with that sentiment, I'm going to offer you some unsolicited advice."

I sucked in a breath. "Okay ... let's have it."

"Be careful."

I squinted at him. "That's it?"

"Well, I'm not sure what else to say. In between Agapios and the wolves, I'm concerned Obsidian won't be able to protect you."

"Can't I depend on the trees for protection?"

He paused. "You could ... if you hadn't hacked a plant nearly to death in a fit of rage. Couldn't you hear it screaming Korrina? The trees tell me it was horrific."

I blanched. "I'm so sorry. I was so out of it, I didn't think. I'll make it right, Uncle Solon. I promise."

He kissed the top of my head. "I know you will, youngling. Just don't let it happen again. The trees are always willing to sacrifice themselves, but take care to ask them first, okay?"

"Yes, sir," I said, not able to look him in the eye. I was embarrassed by the way I'd acted. I'd always prided myself on my connection to the trees. How could I be so distracted by Obsidian and Oswin that I didn't even notice they'd stopped speaking to me? They were as much of a part of me as an arm or leg.

Solon smiled reassuringly. "We've all had our moments of weakness, Korrina. It's what we do after that's important."

I nodded, deep in thought. What if they never forgave me?

Even with Obsidian in my life, I didn't think I could make it without the trees. I needed them to feel like … well, me.

Slipping an arm around my shoulders, Solon said, "Don't worry. They still love you."

"We do love you, child of Dionysus," the trees said in unison. "And we forgive you."

Tears welled up in my eyes. "Thank you," I whispered.

"On that, I think we'll conclude our first secret meeting," Solon said, cranking the car and shifting into reverse. "I better get you home before Obsidian comes looking for you."

I raised my brows. "Does that mean they'll be more mystery meetings to come?"

He pulled out onto the deserted main road and put the car in drive. "Until the wolves go home and Agapios is caught, I think I'll be seeing you pretty regularly."

"Think we could include Obsidian in the next one?"

He winked at me. "If you trust him, I trust him."

TROUBLE AT A BREAKNECK SPEED
OBSIDIAN

Korrina didn't talk much after Solon left. She didn't have to. We both knew what was going through her mind. Putting her fear into words wouldn't help the situation.

"Want to finish the movie?" I asked her. She'd probably feel better if she took her mind off of the problems at hand.

"Not really," she said, her voice small and scared. "Can we cuddle, though? I kind of need a hug right now."

I kicked off my shoes and laid on the couch, holding out my arms. "Come here, love."

She eagerly climbed into my embrace, sighing heavily as she rested her head in the crook of my arm. After a silent minute or so, she said, "When we were in the car, Solon told me you didn't have emotions before you met Edith. Is that true?"

Tucking her hair behind her ear, I breathed in its intoxicating scent and murmured, "Solon wouldn't have said it otherwise."

"What changed you?"

I smiled into her hair. "Typical faerytale stuff. I found love and my cold, dead heart came to life."

She smacked my forearm. "Be serious."

"I am being serious. I was emotionless for seventy or so years. Then I met Edith. And now I have met you. I might as well be human at this point."

"A human, I can deal with. Anything is preferable to satyrs and the majority of male nymphs."

I lifted a brow. Korrina rarely talked about her past experiences. I'd been thankful for it before, but after Solon's mention of Agapios, I was more than willing to hear about them. If anything, it would eliminate any more surprises. "Aren't nymphs encouraged to marry their own race?"

"Only because nearly all of them are racist. It's gotten to a point where it's considered taboo to mate with another species."

"And you think that's wrong?"

She turned over to face me. "Don't you?"

I didn't answer her. "What about the satyrs? Aren't they close to the nymphs?"

"Close? Not even a little bit. They live around us because they are as highly sexual as we are and have a better than average chance of getting laid. But no self-respecting nymph actually takes them as lovers."

"Why not?"

"Because they're assholes. They just want to fuck. There's no promise of any relationship or even friendship. A satyr goes from one female or male to another without any thought whatsoever."

"Why would you risk a public nudity arrest to be with one, then?"

She sighed and shrugged. "Because I wanted to fuck. It had been weeks since I last had sex. And the sex I'd had was with a nymph."

I raised my eyebrows in question.

"Let's just say sex with most nymph males is sad," I suggested.

"Ah, I see. And sex with a satyr?"

The corners of her mouth turned up. "Sex with other supernaturals is infinitely hotter, with the exception of Agapios. He seems to have picked up his personality from the nymphs."

Slipping my hand up her shirt, I traced circles onto her back with my fingers. "You know what I think? I think someone likes the taboo."

Korrina closed her eyes and inched closer to me. "I'm not denying it. Normal is boring. I like sharp teeth, claws, and fur."

"And hooves?" I asked.

Her eyes popped open. "Ass."

I rolled her under me, laughing as I kissed her soft, full lips. "I'm glad you like the taboo because I've got something to show you. Something I should have shown you before I asked you to marry me."

"And that is?"

I hesitated. "Don't be afraid, okay? It could be a little off-putting."

"Just show me, Obsidian," she insisted. "I'm growing old here."

I nodded, blinking my eyes back to the solid black I fought so hard to hide and let my teeth elongate to their natural state. I wanted her to see the real me, without the humanoid mask I put on to keep those around me from being afraid.

"H—how?" she stammered, her eyes traveling from my face, down the strange new muscles in my chest and abdomen, and finally landing on the cock that strained against the fabric of my sweatpants.

"I'm a true vampire, Korrina. This is what I look like. Everything else you've seen is a lie."

Eyes wide, she reached up to touch a finger to the point of a bottom fang then gazed into my eyes. "You are ... mouthwatering."

I looked at her with undisguised hunger. "Right back at you."

"Tell me that again in a few seconds," she said, her expression uncertain. "There's something I want to show you, too."

"Wh—" My words escaped me as I stared at Korrina in fascination. In awe, I watched her skin begin to pale, and her features become slightly angled. Her long dark hair lengthened and came alive with thousands of winding tendrils full of tiny leaves and delicate flowers. The end result was the stuff of make-believe. Striking and sexy, she was the embodiment of nature itself. I couldn't help but wonder if she would taste differently in her true form, if her blood would be more sweet or potent. I licked my lips. "I didn't think it was possible for you to be more beautiful than you were."

She inclined her head toward my crotch. "I didn't think you'd be so proportional."

Chuckling, I carefully pressed my lips to hers, wanting so much to revel in the smell and taste of her, but knowing I couldn't lose myself. With my vampire unleashed, it was harder to control the monster in me, harder to quell the voracious appetite I had for her blood.

Korrina had no such qualms. She fused her mouth to mine the moment our mouths met, all while frantically trying to push down my pants. "Obsidian, work with me here."

I lifted my eyebrows in surprise. "Slow down, Korrina. I don't want to hurt you. It's harder for me to control myself when I'm like this."

Ignoring my warning, she rolled us to straddle me, jerked her panties to the side, and sank down on my erection as soon as it was uncovered, moaning loudly when my girth was almost too much to take.

"I tried to warn you," I growled.

She threaded her fingers in my hair and tugged my head back. "Shut up and fuck me."

With a roar, I slipped my arms underneath her legs and pinned her to the couch, thrusting wildly into her. "Is this what you want?" I asked, licking a path up her jugular.

"Yes," she hissed, flexing her hips.

"Good," I growled. "Because I am never letting you go."

***

Hours later, I lay tangled in the sheets of Korrina's bed. She was in my arms, her breathing even with sleep. She'd shed her nymph appearance when we moved to the bedroom for the sake of convenience; carrying all that hair around had to be rough on her. I, too, went back to my humanistic form soon after, just to get her to take a break from sex. She'd spent most of the night becoming familiar with my body, and as happy as I was about that, I could tell I had exhausted her. When I finally tucked her beside me and begged her to get some sleep, she'd told me I was like chocolate— wholly delicious but too much of a good thing.

I smiled at the memory. A month ago, I couldn't have foreseen this. Being with someone … anyone was unthinkable. I'd given up on having a female in my life after Edith, especially one I could be myself with. Solon changed all of that when he sent Korrina here. Somehow he knew exactly what I, what we, needed. He was always a smart male, that Solon.

***

But just like with all good things that happened in my life, things soon started to fall apart. A few minutes after Korrina fell asleep, a strangled scream sounded next to the house, startling her awake. Springing up from the bed, I held a finger over my lips and shook my head silently as I turned to mist, reappearing moments later with a grim expression and my slacks on.

"What was that, Obsidian?" Korrina whispered.

"Nothing good." I held out my hand. "Come take a look."

Korrina let out an audible gasp as we walked out onto the front porch. Amber Hollick was on the ground just beyond the circle of light coming from the porch light, her head cocked at an impossible angle. "Obsidian, this is the woman from the other night. Is she …"

Yes," I answered quickly, my mind spinning in a hundred different directions. There were no other apparent signs of injury, except for my bite on her neck. It was faint, obviously an old

128

wound, but it was doubtful the Bureau would listen to reason when faced with a dead human on a vampire's land.

Hurrying back inside, I slipped on the shoes I'd left in the living room the night before, while Korrina chewed what was left of her fingernails off. "We have two options," I told her, returning to the porch. "Bury the body and skip the Bureau or call the Bureau and pray they don't stake me."

We both jumped when we heard sirens in the distance. It was too late for options. "Who would do this?" Korrina asked. "What enemies do you have, Obsidian?"

"Just Oswin," I said honestly. "But he wouldn't have done this. He would have made sure you couldn't be implicated. There has to be someone else."

Korrina's face filled with dread. "Oh my God … the pack. It could be any of them. They think I'm going to be the next Alpha female."

I walked further into the yard and took a deep breath. "Call him," I told her. "Tell him to find out who's done this, and tell him you will be his mate. You may need the diplomatic immunity. The Bureau will try every scenario to pin this on us."

Tears streamed from her eyes. "But what about you? What can I do?"

"Tell the truth. Her bite is old, and there is no blood on her body. They'll have nothing against me but the location of her death."

"That's it?" she asked incredulously. "That's not good enough."

The sirens were growing louder. They'd be here in less than three minutes. "Come in the house, Korrina. We don't have much time."

Sniffling, she followed me inside. "Obsidian, I—"

"I know. I love you, too."

Throwing herself in my arms, she said, "This can't be happening."

"Call Oswin," I said, putting her phone in her hand. "Then I'll call the Bureau. It will look better if we call them before they get here."

She dialed his number, and I heard him pick up right away. "Hey, darlin'. Is that sirens I'm hearing?"

Korrina spoke quickly. "We heard a scream outside and found a human dead just past the front porch. Her neck's been broken. Obsidian smells wolves. We didn't call the Bureau, but they are obviously on their way. Someone is trying to frame us, Oswin."

"The pack," Oswin ground out, regret heavy in his voice. "I'm on my way. I'm not far. And I'll call your uncle in Meadowbrook. You said he was a judge, right? Hopefully, he can help us."

She wiped the tears from my cheeks. "Yeah, Solon Manetas."

"All right." He paused for a moment. "Korrina, is there any way Obsidian could have done this?"

"No. We were together when we heard her scream."

He sighed. "I'll do everything I can, Korrina. See you soon."

"Thank you."

Korrina hung up the phone and nodded to me. I was already dialing the Bureau. As soon as the operator picked up, I said, "I'd like to report an unresponsive person at my residence, 819 Sycamore Drive in Goshen. Thank you."

I hung up the phone and kissed Korrina again, this time with bloody tears in my eyes. "We're not together. Do you hear me? You're in my custody, and that's it. I don't want you associated with me. You and Oswin have to look like lovers."

"I understand." She wiped her eyes with her sleeve and straightened her shirt. "I'm ready."

I opened the front door just as the patrol car pulled in the driveway. Two Bureau agents stormed out of their car, guns drawn. "Get down on the ground!"

LOST AND FOUND
OSWIN

I slammed my truck door and turned over the engine. This whole thing was an absolute fucking nightmare. Pulling out into traffic, I was so pissed at myself for being careless that I almost didn't see the elderly pedestrian crossing the street and had to slam on the brakes. After a quick showing of his middle finger, the man hobbled along, and I went back to berating myself. The fact that Korrina had been found meant that I'd been followed on my visits. I'd brought the pack to her doorstep. If the Bureau staked Obsidian, it would be all my fault.

What my pack did was a dirty, underhanded move. Sabotaging the only leverage that could keep me in my position of Alpha was as low as a wolf could go. If they were truly worthy of the title, they would win it in a fair fight—not in this devious manner. But really, when the fuck had my traitorous pack members cared anything for fairness or the fact that innocent creatures would get hauled down to the precinct as murderers. I couldn't let this kind of treachery prevail. Whoever did this had better be enjoying the last breaths they would ever take. Vengeance would be swiftly delivered.

***

I pulled into the Bureau's parking lot precisely one hour after Korrina's call. Her uncle met me at the door of my truck. "Mr. Morris?"

Inclining my head, I shook his hand. "Judge Manetas, I wish we were meeting under better circumstances."

"As do I. I assume you're here to offer Korrina the pack's immunity?"

"I'm offering her more than that. I still want her for my mate."

His eyebrows rose. "Are you aware she has another suitor with a proposal on the table?"

I could feel my wolf's hackles rise beneath my skin. "I am aware that Obsidian Raines is in her life. Has she accepted him?"

"Yes, the last I heard."

I blew out a sigh of aggravation and ignored the engagement announcement. "Have you seen them since their arrest? What are we dealing with?"

"So far, it looks like an accomplice to murder, but they don't have a scrap of evidence connecting either one of them to the crime."

"Good."

"Even without immunity, I could probably get Korrina out on bail," Solon continued. "However, I fear my friend, Obsidian, will be lost to us forever if we can't find the woman's killer soon. Murderers usually go on trial fairly quickly with the Bureau. I'd say we only have a couple weeks before his sentencing."

"We?" I asked. "Why aren't we leaving a murder investigation to the authorities?"

He looked at me with an expression of weary exasperation. "I'm sure at your advanced age you're familiar with the way the Bureau works. They don't investigate vampire murders. They eliminate the suspect, just in case it could ever happen again."

Solon was right. I knew all too well how true his words were. Everyone in the preternatural community did. I had to find out who was behind this. Competition or not, I couldn't let an innocent male die because of my pack and I. "I'll do everything I can," I told him. "I want to make this right."

"See that you do, Mr. Morris. Now, let's go inside. She's been waiting for you." He stopped me as I started for the gate and dropped his voice down to a whisper. "Oswin, you go in there and act like you own the place. Get loud. Demand your bride. They should unhand her immediately after you are verified as pack master. I will act as your lawyer."

I gave him an encouraging smile. "So, be me, right?"

"Right," Solon said chuckling. He motioned for me to get going.

After the gate guards buzzed Solon and me in, I opened the heavy steel door with more force than necessary, letting it bang against the wall behind it. Everyone behind the counter jumped and turned to stare at us as we walked through a mist of plaster dust to the desk. I aimed a grimace at the crowd of Bureau employees with a viciousness that would have given children nightmares as I approached. "My bride," I growled. "Now."

The human employee closest to me pointed a shaky finger at the hallway next to the reception desk. His voice trembled as he spoke. "Right this way, Packmaster."

"Prepare the release papers," I growled at the rest of them. "My betrothed has immunity."

As a flurry of activity began behind us, Solon whispered, "Nicely done."

The guard led us to the end of the hallway and through two more heavy steel doors before coming to a stop outside a closed door with no window. "She's through here, Mr. Morris," he said, punching in a code.

I surveyed the human's face. There was a smugness that wasn't there before, and his tremble had all but disappeared. What had given him courage?

I stepped to the door, and all was revealed. Silver. To a nymph, it meant nothing. To a wolf or vampire, it meant excruciating pain and eventual death. He knew that opening the door would hurt me, and judging by his accelerated heart rate, he got off on inflicting pain.

Leveling a stare at the human, I waited as if I expected to have the door opened for me.

"Allow me, pack master," Solon said, hurrying forward.

I never took my eyes away from the human as I spoke to Solon. "Thank you for your assistance. I will remember it."

Solon followed my glare to the man and smiled nastily. "Packmaster, it is my honor."

The human swallowed hard and practically ran back to the front office. I rolled my eyes at his absurd attempt at a power play and ducked into Korrina's silver prison. She was asleep, her dark hair hiding her face. "Wake up, darlin'. It's time to go."

Her green eyes fluttered open, and she started to cry. "Oswin, please get me out of here."

"It's done, sweetheart. They should have the paperwork ready by now."

She ran into my arms. I held her to my chest, stroking her hair. She was trembling like a leaf. "Thank you."

I chuckled. "You didn't think I'd let you stay here, did you?"

"No, but what about Obsidian?" she asked, pulling away but not looking me in the eye.

I sighed. "I'm working on it. He's not as easy to spring."

Her eyes met mine. They were so full of sadness; I couldn't look away. "We have to try, Oswin. He's innocent."

"We will, darlin', we will." Picking her up bride-style, I carried her out of the cell. "Solon, put her in my truck if they'll allow it. Don't let her out of your sight."

Knowing what I was up to, he nodded. "Of course."

Handing her off, I took a deep breath and followed Obsidian's scent. I found him two cells down the row.

"Oswin?" his weak voice asked. "Is that you?"

"Yeah, it's me. I promise, I'm going to get you out of this. I won't rest until I find the wolf responsible."

There was a long pause before the vampire responded. "Take care of Korrina."

"You don't have to ask it," I told him.

"And when I get dusted, make sure she gets everything of mine. She loves the houses. I want her to have them."

"That's not going to happen, Obsidian."

"Just the same, wolf."

I sighed. "It shall be done, brother."

I left Obsidian and found my way back to the front desk, eager to get back to Korrina. "What do you need from me?" I asked. "I need to get my bride home."

The tiny Fae female behind the desk shivered in fear. "Sign and initial this, and you are free to take Miss Manetas to the pack-lands."

"Thank you for your help," I growled, letting my teeth lengthen into sharp points. She squeaked in answer and fainted. Smiling, I signed and made a quick exit as the others in the room surged in to assist her.

***

Korrina didn't say anything for over an hour after we parted from Solon. She just sat there, hands in her lap, staring out the windshield. I was starting to worry.

"You all right over there?" I asked.

Fresh tears slipped down her cheeks. "I'm fine."

I slowed and pulled the truck to the shoulder. "No, you're not. Come here."

She unbuckled her seatbelt and curled into my side, laying her temple on my chest. "What are we going to do, Oswin?"

"He'll be okay," I said, squeezing her tight. "We'll find a way to set him free."

She buried her face in my shirt. "If he dies, it will be my fault."

"Korrina, it could never be your fault," I told her. And that was the honest to God truth. It was my fault Obsidian was arrested. It was my stupid pride that was going to get someone I'd once considered a brother killed.

When she looked up, I could barely keep my eyes on her sorrowful face. The guilt that look caused was nearly incapacitating. "Promise me, Oswin," she pleaded. "Don't let him die."

I sighed. "I promise, darlin'. I won't let another male die for my pack's offenses."

She lifted her head. "You really think it was the pack?"

"I know it was the pack," I said through clenched teeth.

"How will you punish them for what they've done?"

I stroked her cheek. "I think I'm going to let you choose the punishment. It will be your right as my female."

She looked perversely pleased. "Good. When will we have the ceremony?"

"I will make you my mate tomorrow night if you're ready. It's traditional to do it under the full moon."

"I'm ready," she answered quickly, a manic gleam in her eyes.

I frowned. "Are you sure? You know what this mating will entail, don't you? There will be no going back to Obsidian after we mate. You'll be my female alone, no one else's."

With zero hesitation, she spoke to me with her heart. "Oswin, you are considered a king in our community, and I'm half in love with you already. How could I ever choose a better mate?"

"Well, when you say it like that, I do sound pretty great," I said, grinning down at her.

"You are pretty great," she told me. "You didn't have to do

this for me."

I tipped her chin up and kissed her perfect rosebud mouth. "I didn't just do it for you."

***

I lightly shook Korrina awake an hour later. She had fallen asleep minutes after we got on the highway. Exhausted, she had curled up cat-like against my side, the picture of beauty as she rested. "Korrina, we're here."

Her eyes blinked open, and she sat up. "Is the coast clear?"

I glanced out the windshield and saw two sets of glowing eyes in the bushes. "Nope. Slide out after me, okay?"

She arched an eyebrow and grinned. "Let's do this."

"Easy there, Rambo. Don't get crazy. We don't know if they're friendlies or not."

She laughed. "Okay."

I waited until Scott and Pete stepped out of the shadows to exit the truck. I was taking no chances with my mate.

"Hey, Boss," Pete called, grinning like an idiot at Korrina. "Who's this?"

"This is Korrina Manetas, my soon-to-be mate."

Scott whistled. "Oswin, you didn't tell us she was so beautiful."

I smiled proudly. "She is, isn't she?"

Korrina rolled her eyes. "She's standing right here."

Scott blushed. "Sorry, Ma'am."

"It's okay. And I do appreciate the compliment, but it's just been a really long day."

"I second that," I said. "Guys, I think I need to get this little lady inside."

"We'll be here if you need us," Pete said, yanking Scott back to their post by his collar. "Come on, loverboy. Let's let the lady rest."

Korrina went straight to the bathroom to shower as soon as I let her in the house. I left her to her privacy and went to the kitchen to make some calls for more security. I didn't want to make Korrina a prisoner in my home, but her gung-ho attitude worried me. Her safety was of the utmost importance. The future of the pack depended on it. And she needed to understand that whoever murdered the human might have wanted her to be brought back to the pack- lands for a reason, and that reason could be that she'd be easier to kill here.

***

Korrina appeared in the kitchen wearing one of my t-shirts twenty minutes later. "I borrowed your shirt. I hope you don't mind."

"Borrow anything you like. It will all belong to you tomorrow, anyway."

She smiled distractedly. "So, where do I find my teacups and tea?"

"In the cupboard over the dishwasher, where you left them, remember?"

Laughing, she opened the cabinet. "Oh my goodness!"

I turned to see what had made her exclaim and froze. She held my sister's favorite Flora Danica teacup delicately between her hands.

"Oswin, why do you have a two-hundred-year-old teacup in the cabinet?"

"It was my sister's favorite cup. I always kept it handy for when she came over to visit."

She placed the cup back in the cabinet and frowned. "She doesn't visit anymore?"

"She died a few years ago."

Korrina laid her hand on my arm. "I'm sorry. Was she killed?"

"In a sort, I guess. She grieved over a choice she made many years ago. It consumed her, aged her, until one day, she gave up."

"I didn't know that could happen to a wolf."

"It is very unusual for a werewolf to die in that way, but not unheard of. We are closer to our animal than some of the other Weres."

She stared at the table, deep in thought. "I guess I don't know very much about the wolves … or you."

Gathering her in my arms, I held her close to me and breathed in her clean scent. "You will. In a couple of hours, you'll wish you hadn't accepted my help."

"That's where you're wrong," she said, shaking her head. "I'll always be grateful for your help in my time of need."

I sighed. "We'll see about that. I'm going to shower and then we'll talk, okay?

"Sure."

***

Never one to wait for an appropriate time, Korrina came into the bathroom with her tea just as I was rinsing the shampoo from my hair. I pulled back the curtain a couple of inches. "Is everything okay, Korrina?"

She dawdled a bit before answering. "Why will I regret accepting you, Oswin?"

With a deep sigh, I turned off the faucet and opened the curtain. She handed me a towel. "Darlin', being with an Alpha has strings attached to it. And there are days when the pull of those strings are going to make you feel like a puppet—a puppet at the mercy of this godforsaken pack of mine. You will hate them, as I do, and in time, you will grow to hate me for making you my female."

140

"Are they really as bad as you're making them out to be?"

I stepped out with the towel around my hips and led her to the bedroom. I couldn't lie to her. She'd find out the truth soon enough. "A good majority of them are, yes. They long for the way things were in the past, for the carnage and terror they once rained down upon the humans."

"And that's why they hate you?"

"They hate me because I killed their last Alpha, and with him, those old ways."

She recoiled away from me. "Why?"

"It is customary," I assured her, holding up my hands. "I defeated him in the fight to become Alpha. I grew tired of his abuse toward humans and his insatiable lust for the females of the pack. I killed him to save us from becoming savages."

"Okay. So, does that mean someone can challenge you for Alpha?"

"Yes, and they have, seven times. I hated to lose some of them. It is regrettable that so many oppose what is good."

"You killed all of them?"

"I had to, Korrina. If I didn't, his cohorts would. It's disgraceful to lose a packmaster challenge."

"If you ever do lose, what happens to your mate?"

"It won't happen, but if I'm ever incapacitated or killed, you will have two choices for your future. You can leave the pack, or you can take my place as Alpha—providing you are able to best the one who has defeated me and anyone else who decides to challenge you."

She nodded but said nothing.

I sat on the bed and held out my arms. "Come here and lay with me, Korrina. You need sleep. You're safe here. I promise you. No one in the pack is strong enough to best me."

Still silent, she did as I asked, curling around me and nuzzling her face into my chest.

"I know it's a lot to ask, but try not to worry," I told her. "It won't be all bad. There are still wolves in the pack that will celebrate our mating."

"How many will oppose us?" she asked, peeking up at me.

Her luminous green eyes mesmerized me. "Maybe, twenty-five? Our mating will effectively ruin my opposition's last chance of removing me from my position without a proper challenge. That's sure to piss them off."

She propped up on an elbow. "That's why you said you weren't just doing this for me, isn't it? You're trying to stop them from taking over."

I smiled and shook my head. Would this female never understand the depth of my feelings for her? In my long life, I'd never felt this way about another female. "I want you for my mate, Korrina. That's why I said that. Since the day I met you, you have been everything to me."

She bit her lip. "I know we've had a hard start with Obsidian in the picture, but I want you to know that you can trust me. I won't stray from you."

"Good. I don't want to waste one minute of our mating on jealous thoughts and uncertainty. If you can promise to remain faithful to me, then I promise to do the same."

"I should hope so," she said, raising an eyebrow. "Wolves mate for life, right?"

I laughed. She was right to call me out on it. Her commitment would be a hell of a lot harder than mine would. A virtuous nymph was unheard of. "That's right, so you better be sure you really want to mate me tomorrow."

"I'm positive I want to be your mate. I think you'll be rather easy to love." She cocked her head to the side. "But can you tell me why you're staring at me with that goofy grin?"

"It's called happiness," I told her. "Maybe you've heard of it?" Korrina was so beautiful, so honest. She made me rethink everything I thought I knew about her. I didn't care that she wasn't a wolf or whether this was a reckless move to make. Right now, I just felt lucky to have a second chance to have her in my life.

Eyes narrowed, she climbed up to kiss me. "So we're going to have a monogamous relationship?"

"That's right."

A seductive smile crossed her lips. "Then don't you think we should get started on that?"

Though my dick strained to be inside her, I knew I had to have self-control. "Don't get carried away, darlin'. This is how we got distracted last time we were here, remember?"

Her expression became even more lustful. "Remember? How could I forget? I lie awake at night wondering what would have happened if we hadn't been interrupted by the Bureau."

I knew exactly what she meant. I'd thought about it a hundred times myself. "I still can't believe you came here that night. If you had told me that you were on probation, I wouldn't have let you."

When I noticed the slight pout of her bottom lip, I added, "That's not to say I didn't enjoy the time I did have you here."

Pulling my shirt over her head, she dropped it on the floor. "I enjoyed it, too. I'm looking forward to finding out what will make you mad enough to do it again."

Her enigmatic smile worried me. "I hope not in the same way you did last time."

"Of course not, we're in a monogamous relationship." She started kissing her way down my chest.

"Korrina," I warned. "We have a lot to discuss."

Licking her lips, she looked hungrily at my cock. "So discuss it. I'm listening."

"I can't think when you're looking at my dick like that."

"Close your eyes," she purred. "That way you won't have to watch."

I did as she asked, though I knew she was up to no good and wasn't surprised when I felt her warm mouth envelop me seconds later. "Fuck, Korrina," I groaned, trying hard not to open my eyes. "This is exactly what I meant by distractions," I complained through gritted teeth.

"You know, most males don't protest when I do this."

Leveling my gaze on her swollen mouth, I said, "It's not as if I disapprove, Korrina."

"Then why are you lecturing me while I'm trying to suck your cock?"

"Korrina…" I growled in warning. My wolf was frantically pacing inside of me. The smell of her lust was overwhelming.

Her green eyes glowed in the lamplight. "Yes, Mr. Morris?"

"You're asking for it, darlin'."

"You're wrong, Oswin. I'm begging for it."

I rose up and rolled her onto her back. She smiled knowingly. "Oh, you think you've won, do you?"

She fisted my erection and smiled. "Oh, I know I've won."

"Devious female. How should I punish you?"

Latching a leg around my waist, she rubbed her naked flesh against my hardness. "Use your imagination."

That, I would most definitely do.

THINGS AREN'T LOOKING SO GOOD
KORRINA

October 25th

Oswin snores and whines in his sleep. It's slightly adorable. Hell, he's adorable. But, if I'm being totally honest, I miss Obsidian. Badly. I can't stand the thought of him being locked in that silver prison while I frolic in bed with Oswin like a newlywed. Obsidian giving me his blessing didn't make what I was doing feel any less wrong ... okay, maybe it feels a little right. I mean ... Oswin ... wowwwww.

I'm really fucked up, aren't I?

Don't answer that.

K

After a marathon six hours in bed—mostly horizontal, we decided to make our mating official. I didn't think I could have been more terrified if he had dumped me into a tank full of hungry sharks.

"I'm going to call a pack meeting," Oswin said, lacing his fingers through mine. "It's time I introduce them to their future Alpha female."

I sighed. "Why do I have the feeling it's not going to be as easy as you're making it sound?"

He kissed me then sprung up from the bed in one swift movement. "They'll hate you. You can be sure of that."

"I was already sure of that," I sassed. "Crazy lady-wolf made that very clear the last time I was here."

"Patricia is the least of our troubles," he said, his voice muffled by the sweater he was pulling over his head.

"Who is the most troublesome?"

He pulled on a pair of jeans. "Thom, my second in command."

"If you trust him to be the second in command, why is he troublesome?"

He sat down next to me and took my hand. "I didn't pick him. The second wins the right to the title by defeating their predecessor. I have no say in it. Believe me, he's the last wolf I would have picked."

"Do I need to watch him? If they attack, what do I do? Who are our allies? Can I meet with them first?"

"Whoa. Settle down, Korrina. I'll tell you everything you need to know before we go outside."

I glared at him. His attempt at calming my worries was pathetic. He wasn't taking this nearly as serious as I was. "What the hell, Oswin? I am freaking out here, and you're acting like we're going out for Sunday breakfast. Aren't you scared of their reactions?"

"No."

"How can you not be?"

He smiled a big, toothy grin and half-laughed, half-growled. "I'm the big, bad wolf, Korrina. I am afraid of no one. I didn't become Alpha by fretting about being killed, and you shouldn't either."

As if it was that easy! "Uh, Oswin, I'm not strong like you are or as fast. I'm not a wolf."

It suddenly dawned on me that I was a little jealous of the females of the pack. I would never be accepted like they were, probably would never have a wolf that I could call a best friend here. And I would never be able to give Oswin a pure wolf pup as they could. My assets were far outweighed by my faults. Why would Oswin choose me for something as important as this?

"Nope," Oswin said. "I know that look already. I made my choice, and you're not going to make me change my mind."

I frowned. "Are you sure you wouldn't rather marry a wolf from another pack? I can't give you what they can."

He sighed. "You're so hung up on not being like us that you're forgetting how hard it is to live with us. Hell, you haven't even seen me as a wolf. We're impetuous, argumentative, and we shed."

I laughed. "Great. Now I'm dying to see it. Are you up for showing me?"

"Sure," he said.

His response seemed chipper enough, but a brief look of foreboding crossed his features just after his answer. Was this transformation painful for him? Had I just asked him to hurt himself? He moved the couch and motioned for me to back up. "Wait!"

"What is it?"

"Are you one of those werewolves that have to be naked or do your clothes just magically disappear and reappear?"

He shook his head, his face full of confusion. "What? Where do you come up with this stuff?"

"TV."

"You could just ask me."

"That's what I'm doing!"

He shook his head again and pulled off his shirt and jeans. "Get ready."

I nodded. "Okay."

With a loud crack, his torso jerked to the floor, and a howl erupted from his mouth, which was fast becoming a muzzle. Howls and yips followed his from the wolves outside and grew deafeningly loud until a crescendo was reached. Then, absolute silence. Even I couldn't make a sound. I was rendered speechless by the sight of Oswin as a huge silver wolf.

It was incredibly easy to see why Oswin was Alpha. He was easily three times the size of an ordinary wolf. Whining, he padded to me tentatively, his massive head facing down. He wouldn't meet my eyes.

"Wow," I murmured, burying my face into his chest and threading my fingers through the fur on either side of his neck, though I had to stand on the tips of my toes to do it. He nudged me closer with a giant paw, and I smiled to myself. I didn't think I could really love him, not while Obsidian was in my heart, but it was there; I loved him. "Oswin, I think we're going to need a bigger bed. This fur is going to keep me warm in this frigid house."

He barked out an almost normal laugh and began to shrink beneath my hands. I backed away and watched his transformation into the male I knew.

"That's really cool."

"Cool?" He grinned. "I thought you'd be frightened."

I giggled. "Of you? No way! Can I ride you?"

Eyes still yellow, he answered with a ravenous smile. "You want a ride, little nymph?"

He scooped me up, kissed me, and then groaned. "We have incoming." Setting me on my feet, he cautiously stepped to the door and sighed. "Get dressed. The pack is here."

Leaving him to deal with our unexpected company, I went in search of clothes. I wondered if he had kept the overnight bag that I'd left here before. We hadn't exactly got around to washing the clothes I wore last night.

I spied the bag underneath a chair and quickly pulled on jeans, a t-shirt, and a pair of flats. Once dressed, I made my way back to the living room. I could hear familiar bickering through the front door but didn't join Oswin out there. I didn't want to aggravate the situation by interrupting something important, like Oswin's concentration on not killing Patricia. I could practically hear his teeth grinding above her shrill voice.

Holding my ear to the wall, I tried to overhear what Oswin was saying.

"Patricia, calm yourself—now. As Alpha, I'm entitled to choose my mate. It has always been so."

"She is an abomination!" Patricia spat.

My eyebrows raised. Abomination? That was pushing the envelope just a bit, wasn't it?

"Hold your tongue, or I will cut it out!" Oswin growled angrily.

"I'll say what I like. And if that whore were here, I'd tell her to her face!" she shouted in defiance.

If that wasn't my cue to enter, I didn't know what was. Taking a deep breath, I prayed it would quiet my pounding heart and grasped the doorknob. I slung it open with a crash, making everyone jump. I knew by the look of amazement on Oswin's face and the look of fear on the wolves' faces that they'd never seen a nymph in the flesh before.

"Hello," I said sedately, enjoying their looks of awe when the many trees around the house echoed me.

Recovering quickly, Oswin smiled approvingly at the males who bowed at their waist and returned my hello then frowned at Patricia, who, true to form, continued to sneer at me.

Angry, I took Oswin's arm and looked up to him. "Oswin, my mate, I have often wondered what would happen to sour grapes if they were left to fester and rot. I was right to think that the result would be something nasty."

Complete silence. You could have heard a pin drop.

That is until the trees broke out into helpless giggles. They shook so hard that they littered the front yard with hundreds of leaves and pinecones.

With a roar, Patricia launched herself at me, only to be dragged off screaming by the vines that had snaked around her legs while she wasn't paying attention. We followed her out into the yard, her screams reverberating around the clearing.

Oswin tucked me under his arm. "That was awesome," he whispered.

I shrugged and looked at the dangling she-wolf over our heads. "I just hope they let her down."

We watched Patricia struggle with the vines until she gave up. By that time, most of the pack was gathered in the clearing and were all talking over one another. Oswin stepped up onto his porch with me and spoke over the din. "Today, I announce my choice for a mate. I do not need to remind you that if you harm my choice, it will result in a punishment of my choosing—or in Patricia's case, a punishment of my mate's choosing."

All eyes targeted me. I waved. "Hi, I'm Korrina."

Pandemonium broke out. Four or five wolves rushed the front porch, only to be stopped by security that came out of nowhere. Oswin grabbed me and slung me over his shoulder to deposit me into the front seat of his pickup. "Wait here." He spoke to one of the guards, who turned away and went into the house immediately. To the others, he gave a command, and they spread out in front of the truck and house.

"Aaron, Ethan, Patricia, Darrell, and Ross, you are under arrest for the attempted murder of the future Alpha female," Pete said.

Angry voices yelled out in protest.

"Silence!" Oswin boomed.

The trees, ever listening, decided to release Patricia at that moment. I'm guessing for emphasis. I cringed as I heard her body fall loosely to the ground with a thump. Even for a wolf, a twenty-foot fall was pretty bad.

Or maybe not. As soon as the guards lifted her to her feet, her eyes found mine. If looks could kill, I'd be a spot on the passenger side seat right now.

Oswin poked his head into the cab of the truck, my purse in his hand. "Go visit Obsidian. Give me a couple hours to get things settled."

I leaned to kiss him. "Okay, but I think it went really well."

Incredulous seemed too tame of a word for his expression. "How can you say that? Five wolves tried to attack you today."

"Yes, but fifty didn't. That's got to count for something."

"Maybe," he responded, before tapping the hood twice and walking away.

***

Obsidian was escorted into the visitation room with a stake aimed at his chest. He barely noticed it. He barely saw me. There was none of the smirks or bravado that I was used to, only a distant look in his black eyes.

Saying nothing, the officers shoved him into the hard steel chair across from me and left us alone. He drew his dead eyes up to mine. "My love, you are radiant."

"I wish I could say the same," I said, noticing how shaken he seemed. It appeared the silver in his cell was taking its toll a lot faster than I'd hoped. "Are they treating you well? Have you eaten?"

"I haven't seen anyone since I've been here. I haven't even been questioned yet."

That was not a good sign. Solon had been right. They had no intention of ever letting him go. I held out an arm. "Feed from me."

"You don't have to. I'll be fine for a couple days. Besides, your betrothed wouldn't approve."

"My betrothed doesn't tell me what I can and can't do. I want

151

you to eat." When he still wouldn't budge, I bit my lip and kissed him.

He smiled weakly and licked the blood off his lips. "Glad to see you haven't changed."

"Did you really expect me to? It's been less than a day since I saw you last."

"I don't know what to expect, except death. I know I'm not getting out of here. I'm just glad Oswin was able to get you immunity. It was killing me knowing that you were in here because of me."

I rolled my eyes. "Don't be such a martyr. I was in here because of the pack, not you."

"You know this for a fact?"

"Maybe. Why don't you eat, and I'll tell you all about it?"

"Are you trying to bribe me?"

I scoffed. "Trying, hell, I'm doing it."

He shook his head. "You're unbelievable."

"Don't I know it. Now, quit stalling and eat."

Reluctantly, he bit into the wrist I offered, never taking his cold eyes off of mine. I ran the fingers of my free hand through his dark hair. "I'm going to miss this ... and you. Will you visit the pack-lands, Obsidian?"

He licked the bite wound closed and pulled my mouth to his, lingering for a moment. "The wolves would never allow me on pack grounds, Korrina. But, none of that matters. I'm never leaving this place."

"Yes, the hell, you will," I said with conviction. "And you don't have to worry about that pack-lands rule. It's changed."

"Oh?"

"Yeah, two seconds ago."

He frowned. "Shouldn't you run that by your mate?"

"If he has a problem with it, I won't become his mate. I need you in my life, Obsidian. I won't give up your friendship. I have to give up everything else, but I won't give up what we have for each other in our hearts."

"Will you be happy with him?" he asked, crushed by my words. We both knew how close I'd been to becoming his wife. Now our chance was gone forever.

I hesitated. Honesty just did not seem like the best policy here. It would only hurt him.

"The truth, Korrina."

I started to cry. "The truth is … I like him. And he loves me. It's not the same as it is between us, but there could be something there."

Surprisingly, he looked relieved. "I'm glad. I didn't want you to have to do something you'd regret."

"Do you really mean that … the glad part?"

"Fuck no. I want to rip the guard's throats out, escape, and marry you."

"You want more honesty?"

He stroked his knuckle across my cheek. "Hit me, love."

"I wish you could do just that."

He glanced at the door. "They're coming back. I love you, Korrina."

I pressed my lips to his and whispered, "I love you. And I will get you out of here. I have to, for my own sanity."

"It would be easier to forget about me. Oswin deserves your full attention."

I pursed my lips. "When have you ever known me to take the easy route, Obsidian? This is the only way I can live with this. Please, let me be selfish with this one thing."

"If it keeps you in my life, you know I can't say no."

We heard the lock disengage a second before the guards spilled in. Predictably, they were unnecessarily rough when they pulled Obsidian up out of his chair. I glared at all of them, memorizing their faces. They would pay for the way they treated the male I loved.

Halfway back to Thomasville, I decided that I couldn't ignore the relentless need to go to Meadowbrook anymore. Free of all my restrictions, I could technically go home whenever I wanted. And right now, I needed answers like nobody's business. Thank God Solon was a virtual wealth of sage advice and knowledge.

I pulled over, put the truck into park, and dialed Oswin's phone. I crossed my fingers he wouldn't get mad.

"Hey, darlin'. I was just about to call and ask how it went with the vampire."

I sighed. "He's all right, but they haven't questioned him yet. He said he hadn't seen a soul since his arrest."

"Hadn't seen a soul, huh? That doesn't sound too good. Are they feeding him at all?"

"No."

"Did you?" he asked, his voice tight with emotion.

"If I say yes, will you be angry?"

"No, sugar. I expected you to. You wouldn't let anyone starve if you could help it."

"How are things going over there?" I inquired, hoping it would distract him from the subject.

"Things are … getting settled. The wolves that attacked you have been locked up, and the females of the pack are decorating the ceremonial circle for the mating. Where are you?"

"The side of the road."

"Is the truck broke down? Are you all right?"

"I'm fine. Just feeling a little homesick. Do I have time to go to Meadowbrook before the mating thing?"

"Of course you do. Visit your family. I'll be here when you get back. Just make sure you're here before midnight, or you're grounded."

I giggled. "Yes, sir. Thank you for this, Oswin."

"There's no thanks necessary. You're not a prisoner here."

Oswin was such a good male. One, I wasn't sure I deserved. "I think I love you," I told him.

There was a pause. "I like that."

"I like you."

"I love you too, nymph. Hurry home to me."

"Will do. I'll call you when I get ready to leave."

"I'll be waiting."

"Bye." I threw the phone on the seat and pulled back onto the road, anxious to see my family for the first time in months.

GOING HOME
KORRINA

The moment I pulled into Meadowbrook, the community began to pour out of their houses, all in various shades of undress. No doubt the trees announced my impending arrival. Shaking my head, I steered my way past the crowds, pulled into Solon's driveway, and shifted the truck into park.

My uncle appeared before I could even step out of the truck. "Have you had the ceremony yet?" he asked, whispering so he wasn't overheard.

"Tonight," I answered, taken aback.

He glanced over the hood at Mr. and Mrs. Trakas. They were crouched down behind the hedge trying to hear our conversation. "You can see yourself back inside to the warmth of your home. She has every right to be here."

Mr. Trakas stood up and sneered in my direction. "It's only been a month or less since she was cast out. That's a bit short of five years, Solon."

I climbed out of the truck and walked around. "Hello, Mr. and Mrs. Trakas. How are you?"

They didn't dignify me with a response. That kind of pissed me off.

Smiling sweetly, I said, "If you doubt my right to be here, you're welcome to consult my mate, the Alpha of the Thomasville pack, about it."

"You've mated Oswin Morris?" Mrs. Trakas asked in disbelief.

"I have." I turned back to Solon. "Can we go inside?"

"Sure."

156

"Thanks," I whispered. "With all this commotion, Mom will probably be here in ten minutes. Mrs. Trakas has a huge mouth."

"Make that five minutes. Your mother learned how to text."

Groaning, I set my things down on the hallway table and walked straight into the library. As I suspected, Solon had several books on werewolves, and vampiric law already pulled off the shelves.

"I thought you might come by," he said, observing me.

I fingered the gold lettering on the binding of one of the law books. "I visited Obsidian a couple of hours ago."

"Did you? How is he?"

"Physically, he's okay. Emotionally, I think he's already convinced that he will be staked." I sniffed. "They haven't questioned him at all, Solon."

Dismayed, he sat down in his favorite chair and started packing his pipe with tobacco. "That is bad news."

I tried to fight the tears back, but couldn't. "I can't let him die!" I wailed. "This is my fault. If I hadn't gone out with Oswin to make him jealous, none of this would have happened."

He calmly handed me his handkerchief. "Korrina, stop. We're going to figure out something. We won't let him die."

"We have to. I can't live without him."

He set down his pipe and patted the chair next to him. "No more crying. If you're going to be mated tonight, we should look up some customs." He handed me a thick book. "You read. I'll make tea before your mother gets here."

***

Surprisingly, my mother never showed. Unsurprisingly, there were a million and one wolf laws and customs to learn. If I studied all year, I still wouldn't remember half of what was in the books. I snapped the one in my hand closed and laid my head on the back of the chair, just as Solon came in with the second pot of tea.

He laughed at my exasperated face. "It is a little daunting, isn't it?"

"There are thousands of rules. I can't remember all of this."

"No, you can't," he said, handing me a cup. "Not tonight, anyway. It took me decades."

"You know all this stuff? Why didn't you say so? I bet you already know exactly what I'm looking for!"

He sipped his tea and perched the cup on the arm of his chair. "That depends on what you want to know."

I thought for a moment. "Is there anything in the rules about the Alpha marrying outside his species?"

"Yes. As a matter of fact, it's encouraged. The laws specifically mention the possible benefits of expanding the gene pool to include other magical creatures. Continual inbreeding causes a multitude of problems within pack animals."

"Ewww."

"Precisely my thoughts, I can assure you."

"What about the mating ceremony itself? What do I need to know about that?"

Solon fidgeted—actually fidgeted.

"What is it?" I asked, alarmed. I'd never seen him without his calm composure.

"The mating, in my opinion, is distasteful."

I closed my eyes for a long moment. This would be bad. I could feel it. "How so?"

Without looking me in the eye, he explained. "The mating begins in a circle surrounded by the wolves of the pack. You'll exchange vows and rings as you would in a normal human or nymph ceremony, but immediately after, you will be expected to consummate the marriage … inside the circle."

"In front of the pack?"

"Yes."

"What if you don't do that part?" Loose moral fiber or not, there was no way I could have sex in front of the pack.

"The mating will be considered invalid. It must be done. However, nothing is keeping you from using your magic to cover yourself. The audience does not need to see your first mating for it to be official."

"That's a relief."

"It's best to remember that most of their rules can be interpreted to your liking. There is always a way around things … and really, what good is being the Alpha female if you can't shake up that stagnant pack a bit."

"I don't know, Solon. I think I shook them up pretty good earlier today."

He sighed. "What happened?"

"I swear I didn't have a thing to do with it." I held up my hands innocently. "It was the trees. They were protecting me."

"From whom?"

"The Wicked Witch of the South, Patricia. She hates me. She and some others who tried to rush the house after Oswin announced our mating were arrested today. It was a very eventful afternoon."

Solon seemed to struggle with a response. "Oswin's reputation isn't sparkling, but it is obvious that he has been a better Alpha to the pack than the predecessor. I assume he took care of the threat."

"Yes. He sent me to see Obsidian while he dealt with them."

"Indeed? Well then, he sounds like a decent male. Does he know of your love for the vampire?"

"He is a very good male, and yes, he does."

"I doubt he approves of it."

"I know he doesn't."

"So where does that leave Obsidian when he is free, and you are semi-happily mated?"

I knew what he was asking. Would I remain faithful? "I will be faithful to Oswin, but I refuse to let Obsidian go. I can't."

He arched a disbelieving brow. "Excuse me?"

"We discussed it today. We aren't ready to be apart."

"Will you ever be ready to let him go, Korrina? You need to be sure before you commit to this mating."

"I'm committed to Oswin, one hundred percent. Obsidian understands that."

"I hope he does. I don't believe Oswin is the type of wolf that will agree to share his female in any capacity.

"He won't have to. Obsidian is no threat."

"Hmmm … we'll see."

"Solon, I promised I would be faithful. I intend to keep that promise, regardless of my feelings for Obsidian." I started to pace, keeping my eyes glued to the swirling colors of the Persian carpet. I knew Solon wouldn't approve. Nymphs didn't have monogamous relationships. They just didn't. Even my own parents took the occasional lover when they so desired.

Looking up, I noticed a strange expression on my uncle's face. Surprise wasn't an emotion that my uncle often wore. Actually, I wasn't sure if I'd ever seen the expression on him before now. I stopped in front of him. "Are you okay?"

"Yes, youngling." He gave me a warm smile. "Do you realize how rare it is for one of us to love at all, let alone how rare it is to be able to remain faithful to a lover who is not the one you love?"

"I can't help it," I confessed. "When I think of not having Obsidian in my life, I can't breathe."

"I understand."

"Do you? You don't think I'm being selfish?"

"No, Korrina. I don't."

Smiling stoically, I glanced at the clock. It was getting late. "I guess mom isn't coming. I should be getting back." I motioned to the books. "Can I keep these for a little while?"

"Of course. You'll tell Oswin that I said congratulations on his fine choice in a mate, won't you?"

I beamed and hugged him. "I'd be happy to."

We walked to Oswin's truck as silently as possible, afraid we'd have a reoccurrence of the earlier drama. Kissing me on the cheek, Solon opened the door for me and held my books as I climbed in. "Don't be a stranger, Korrina."

"I won't," I said, cranking the engine and hefting the books to the passenger side.

He shut the door and smiled. "Drive safe, and call me in the morning to let me know how it went."

"I will," I called, backing out of the driveway. "I love you."

He waved. "Love you, too, honey. Good luck."

The pack females had certainly made the meadow into something worthy of an Alpha's mating ceremony while I was away. The empty space in front of Oswin's home had been enchanted. Torches lit along the path and mating circle illuminated vines of flowers draped over every low hanging branch and fence post in sight. Low-lying fog gave it an almost ethereal beauty.

I stood staring in awe until Oswin spoke up from behind me. "They really outdid themselves, didn't they?"

"It's fit for a queen," I said absentmindedly.

He pulled me against his chest and kissed my neck. "It's fit for you."

Facing him, I stood on my toes to kiss his lips. "Thank you."

A worried look crossed his features, and he glanced off into

161

the distance. "We have a little time before we get started. We should talk a little about the ceremony … so you'll know what to expect."

"You don't have to sugar coat it, Oswin. I know about the literal mating part."

Although he was taken aback, he was obviously relieved. "I didn't know how to tell you. Did your parents tell you before th— ?"

"Uncle Solon," I interrupted. "He gave me the gist of it while I was there."

"Are you okay with it?"

"Yes. But, um, you aren't going to be in wolf form, right?" That particular fear had been plaguing me ever since Solon told me of the ritual. I just couldn't bring myself to ask him.

"No, no, darlin'. If you were my species, I would. It is the traditional way."

"Good." I breathed out a sigh of relief. "So, tell me. How do you feel about all the males getting a show tonight?"

He smiled wickedly. "They will be beside themselves with envy. You are a sight to behold when you are naked."

"Flattery will get you everywhere with me, Mr. Morris."

Sliding his hands under my shirt, he skimmed his palms along the bare skin. "Is that right?"

"Oh, yes," I whispered seductively. "I'm actually thinking public sex in front of your pack might be a good reward for that compliment."

He chuckled. "That is a good choice."

"I thought you might approve."

"I have a gift for you inside the house," he said, cupping my face to kiss me.

I trailed my finger down his chest. "A gift? Let me guess. Is it long, thick, and hard?" I bit my lip as I watched him adjust himself then blushed when he caught me watching.

He moved the hair from my shoulder and kissed his way across the column of my throat, before capturing my stare with his. "You know, I've never thought of him as a gift before, but I'm always open to new nicknames."

His wolfy focus was so intense; I couldn't look away from his yellow eyes. "Uh …" I said, stumbling over my next words. "Wh-what do you call him now?"

"Right now, I call him rock hard for you."

I grazed my fingers over the subject at hand. "I like it," I teased. "It suits him."

He glanced down at his erection and frowned. "Yes, it certainly does."

"Then why are you looking at your dick like it's disappointed you?" I asked.

"Because your parents might become disenchanted with the gentlemanly wolf they've come to know over the past four hours if I come in with this."

"There's a gentlemanly wolf here?"

He narrowed his eyes. "Sass will get you everywhere with me, little nymph."

"Tell me something I don't know. Are my parents really here?"

"If your dad is a pompous ass and your mom is a shrill bitch, then yes, your parents are here."

Boy, did he perfectly nail that one on the head. "Oh, yeah. That's them, all right. What the hell are they doing here, Oswin?"

"Solon hates us, and he gave them our address to torture us?" he suggested.

I giggled loudly and slapped a hand over my mouth, praying

my parents hadn't overheard.

"Your father has repeatedly made it known that it is an insult not to have been consulted for the right to mate you," he told me. "Your mother hasn't been as vocal. She's only told me five or six times how much she hates everything here, including me. Have I mentioned they've been here for four hours?"

"Are they pissed at me?" My parents never left Meadowbrook. I had no doubt my old-fashioned father was only here because he wanted some kind of payment for my hand in marriage.

He nodded. "If I remember correctly, I believe the term was 'beyond pissed'."

"Shiiiiit," I said. "Hold my hand, Oswin. That way, when my mother goes batshit, I can make sure you're in the line of fire instead of me."

"How chivalrous, Korrina," he stage-whispered. "Throw me to the wolves, why don't you?"

LAST RESORTS
OSWIN

I felt sorry for Korrina. Really, I did. To have been parented by the two morons that sat in front of me, what a nightmare. And it could not be clearer that Korrina had dealt with this kind of presumptive behavior from them before. I watched in interest as she pushed precisely the right buttons to make them more amiable toward me. So far, all of those buttons were making loud cha-ching sounds, but I was impressed with the way she maneuvered them nonetheless.

When her mother suggested monthly stipends, I took pity on her. I stood up and made a show of glancing out of the window. "Korrina, you should get ready for the ceremony. I'm sure your parents understand that you want to look your best on your mating day."

Catching on quickly, she nodded. "Yes, you're right, I do. Sorry guys, I've got to hurry if I want to make it on time."

They waved her off. They were so eager to make a deal that they were barely listening, anyway. The lengths they were willing to go to for financial gain was appalling.

Patiently, I waited for her to leave the room. Then I turned on them and smiled a malicious grin, dripping with hatred. They were understandingly uncomfortable with the many teeth I displayed in doing so.

"Mr. and Mrs. Manetas, you have exactly twelve seconds to get out of my house and off the pack's land." I glanced at my nonexistent watch. "Starting ... now."

"Or what?" Korrina's father asked incredulously. He seemed unwilling to leave without something to show for their trip.

I took a menacing step toward him. "Or I will eat you," I told him.

My little threat had the desired reaction. Twelve seconds later, they were spinning out of the driveway at a breakneck speed.

Korrina poked her head out of the kitchen and looked around. "Are they gone?"

"Yeah. I've got to tell you, I'm a little disappointed. I thought they'd put up more of a fight."

Shrugging, she straddled my legs, settling into my lap as pantless as the day she was born. "Nymphs aren't territorial like you. They're really just opportunists if anything."

"Hmm…" I said, grabbing her bare ass to pull her against my straining cock. "Opportunists, eh?"

She laughed and pecked me on the mouth. "Thanks for taking care of that."

"I can't believe those are your parents." I mock shuddered. "You're nothing like them."

"Just because parents are supposed to be good, doesn't mean they will be, Oswin."

"That sure is a nice way to look at it, and I really wish I could do the same, but I'm having a bit of trouble overlooking how your parents were complete assholes to you."

"I don't think I could mate you if you didn't. I'm not blind to it, just over it, you know?"

"I do. My parents weren't any better."

"Really?"

"Korrina, I killed my father in the fight to become Alpha … and then defeated my mother when she challenged me directly after."

She jerked her wandering gaze to mine. "Your father was the Alpha?"

I nodded.

"That's awful, Oswin. Were you able to spare your mother's life?"

"Yes, though she killed herself when I refused to do it." I ignored her horrified cringe and plowed forward. "I know all of this must sound terrible to you, but you have to understand that no matter how awful it was on the day of their deaths, it will never be as awful as the way things were in the pack during their rule. Corruption, rape, murder—these were all commonplace occurrences in those days. Trust me, the wolves are much better off without them, and we all know it ... whether or not some of us want to admit it."

She squeezed my forearm. "I'm really sorry you had to go through that."

"If I have any regrets about it at all, it's that I didn't do it sooner. So many wolves and humans were hurt because we were all too afraid to do anything about it for so damn long."

"What made you finally do it? What was the catalyst?"

"My sister. The way they treated her when she married outside of our species was reprehensible. They went out of their way to convince her that she'd made an irreversible mistake in not marrying one of our cousins then forbade her from ever coming back to the pack-lands again. She was never the same after that and eventually died after decades of misery. The day she died was the day I challenged my father."

"I don't know how you do this, Oswin." She shook her head as if she was trying to remove the thought of my sister from her mind. "You had to do the unthinkable to give them a better life, and they hate you for it. You're a saint."

Pulling her head back by her hair, I curved my tongue around a hardened nipple through her shirt and smiled when it elicited a low moan from her lips.

"A saint, huh? You couldn't be farther from the truth, darlin'."

She didn't respond in words, only in the subtle movements of her hips and the rise and fall of her breasts as she inhaled quickened breaths. It would be stupid not to take advantage of her eagerness. She was so ready for me.

Licking up the length of her neck, I brought us face to face. "Korrina, are you ready to fuck me in front of a crowd full of strangers?"

"Wherever you want me, Oswin. I just want you inside of me."

I used a sharpened fingernail to cut the front of her shirt open, letting the scrap of material fall to the floor. "I want to see you like I did this afternoon, Korrina. You were so beautiful. I'd never seen anything like it."

She blushed slightly at my comment but didn't let it deter her from pulling my t-shirt over my head. "I wasn't sure you'd want me like that. I look more human this way."

"I showed you mine," I reminded her. "Now I want to see yours."

She shrugged. "Okay, you asked for it."

The transformation only took a moment. One second, she looked like a beautiful human. The next, she was something altogether different. Her face was pale and angled in an almost alien way, her eyes a bright glowing green. The hair that had hung low on her back now touched the floor and was covered with living, moving vines.

"Korrina, you look like something from a storybook."

She frowned. "That's just what every nymph wants to hear when she's about to get fucked."

I chuckled. "I didn't say it wasn't hot."

"Then take your pants off, wolf, or I will rip them off for you."

"Easy there," I growled. "Save it for the mating."

"Make me," she dared, looking for trouble.

Bucking her off my lap, I slipped the legs of my jeans over my feet and called, "Here I come, little nymph."

She squealed and high-tailed it out the front door, her hair bursting into bloom and making a trail of slowly fading petals for me to follow.

After a moment, I stalked after her, letting her get almost to the ceremonial circle before I caught up to her and secured her arms behind her back. "Ready, darlin'?"

"Yes." With confidence, she took her place in the center of the circle, not sparing the many wolves assembled around the perimeter a glance. I respected the hell out of her for not giving them the satisfaction of knowing she was afraid.

I joined her in the circle, immediately commencing with my vows. "Korrina Manetas of the Meadowbrook nymphs, in the ways of the wolf and the ways of the pack, I pledge myself to you for the remainder of my life."

With my grandmother's ring safely on her hand, Korrina spoke up with her own vow. "Oswin Morris of the Thomasville pack, I pledge myself to you, body and soul." She met the eyes of everyone present before she continued. "No creature, wolf, or man will ever divide us."

I smirked at the pack's angry faces. The challenge issued was clear. She was letting them know that she wouldn't be manipulated by the pack or anyone else while she was my female. She wouldn't be a pawn in the sick game they played—no matter who it pissed off.

"Are you ready?" I asked, eager to get her inside.

She leaned her head back onto my chest and exhaled, "Oswin, please. I need you."

Wasting no time, I maneuvered her to all fours, ignoring the scathing comments from the assemblage when I pushed roughly into her. They were understandably upset. The females because of the rough way I'd taken her, the males because of her origin or her changing our mating vows.

Then, Korrina uttered her first moan of pleasure. After that moment, every spectator stood transfixed as they watched her take what I gave her and beg me loudly to give her more. I couldn't have been more proud of my mate.

When her soft cries became screams, my wolf's instinct told me it was time to mark her. My claiming bite would hurt her so much less that way. I pressed my lips to the crook of her neck before sinking my teeth in. She screamed at the intrusion and in orgasm, dragging me over the edge with her.

When it was all over, she weakly collapsed onto her elbows. To the others around us, it would appear as if the mating had been too much for her, but I knew better. This was something Korrina had planned. She wanted the wolves to underestimate her. She was a smart girl, this one.

Easing out of her, I got to my feet and helped her off the ground. She leaned her limp body against me and asked me to carry her. Without another word to the pack, I hefted her into my arms and took my bride inside to shower. Anything the pack had to say would have to wait until our mating night was over.

***

Korrina didn't take a breath until we were alone in the kitchen. Once there, she sighed in relief. "That was weird, but it wasn't as bad as I thought it would be."

"I'll say it was weird. You just took modern mating to a whole new level. I'm pretty sure you're the first female to orgasm during their ceremony."

She rolled her eyes. "Are they going to be offended about that, too? Because that's more your fault than mine."

"Right now, I don't think there's a male in this pack without an erection. They'll be busy trying to find a place to mate with their females for the next few hours, but we'll most certainly hear about that tomorrow."

"So, you're saying we have a little time to ourselves?"

"Yes," I said reluctantly. "What are you up to?"

"Put me down. I'll show you."

She sank to her knees to take my still throbbing cock in her mouth when I lowered her to the floor. "Korrina," I said, through gritted teeth. "Don't you want to take a shower first?"

"I want you hard and inside of me, Mr. Morris."

I picked her up off the floor and tossed her onto the table. She let out a high-pitched squeak. "You shall have your every whim, Mrs. Morris."

"Oswin!" she exclaimed. "What are you doing?"

I grabbed her ankles and pulled her to the edge of the table. "Giving you what you asked for, darlin'." Leaning forward, I pressed myself against her moist flesh and enjoyed the pleasured shudder that ran the length of her body. "This is what you wanted, isn't it?"

"Yes, please," she said meekly.

Smiling like the cat that ate the canary, I positioned myself at her entrance and thrust hard. Who was I to deny my mate when she'd even said please?

***

The next morning was a shit-storm. There was a dozen or so missed calls on my phone, and no less than twenty-five letters of condemnation slipped under the welcome mat when I woke. The consensus was that there would be hell to pay for our mating last night and that hell would be starting first thing this morning. The honeymoon was apparently over.

Korrina wrapped her arms around me from behind, making me jump. She was very quiet, moving through the house like a ghost. "Make a noise, sugar. You're going to give me a heart attack."

"Come back to bed," she purred. "You can have your heart attack while I'm riding your dick."

I grinned. My favorite thing about my new mate, so far, was that she didn't mince her words. Well, that, and she was always ready for sex. "Sorry babe, we have trouble brewing."

She groaned and went to the cabinet for a coffee cup. "Already? What's going on?"

I tossed the bundle of letters over to her and waited for the reaction I knew would be coming.

"Oh, hell no! Fuck this, Oswin. Point this bitch out to me right now. I'll make sure she'll never be able to pick up another pen."

I laughed. "There's the tactful response I was waiting on."

She wasn't amused. "She called me a whore, Oswin."

"She sure did. You were so beautiful last night. It's just jealousy."

"Whatever."

"Well, then what will you do about it, Mrs. Alpha female?"

She tapped her chin. "Bury her in a shallow grave?"

"No, you'll ignore it."

She set her cup down and spoke very slowly. "If you think, for one minute, that I will allow these wolves to call me names and get away with it, you are sadly mistaken."

"I'll call a meeting tonight to admonish the pack for interrupting what is supposed to be a silent ceremony and for the nasty letters and voicemails. You will then blush and semi-apologize for not being able to control yourself when your extremely well-endowed mate gave you the fucking of your life."

Her mouth dropped open. "Are you kidding me?"

"Nope." I stood and took the letter from Korrina. "It's all a game with this pack. Don't you understand that yet? Most of these wolves are waiting for the moment when someone will challenge me, so they can move up the food chain. It's all the males ever think about. It's the way of the wolves."

"What about you?" she asked, sliding her ankle up my leg.

I grabbed her ankle and trapped her against the counter. "Of course. I'm the reigning Alpha, aren't I?"

"I like it when you're like this," she said softly, running her hands over her naked breasts.

I sniffed the air. She was so very ready for me. "Like what, little nymph?"

She raised her eyes to mine. "A wolf."

I growled low into her ear. "I don't know how to be anything else."

That couldn't be truer—especially now. My wolf was torn between preening for his mate and worrying about the cars he could hear a quarter mile down the road. Apparently, the pack had worked up the courage to face me in person. "We're about to have company, darlin'. They're about a quarter mile out."

She whimpered and put her hands around my erection, urging me to take her. "Isn't there some kind of honeymoon period after you get mated?" she asked. "If I'm fucking my mate when they get here, they can wait."

I jerked a chair out from under the table and sat down. "Fuck 'em."

With a sly, seductive smile, she climbed into my lap and quickly impaled herself on my waiting sex. She was almost unbearably tight, still swollen from our last round only twenty minutes ago. "So good," she whispered, deliberately riding me at a slow, consistent pace.

I closed my eyes, trying hard to keep my wolf at bay. Korrina knew her limitations far better than I did, but I still worried I might hurt her and was trying to be as gentle as I could. Of course, that would be infinitely easier if she didn't insist on tempting my wolf. She'd already learned if she wanted my cock, all she had to do was appeal to him. He didn't have the same concerns for her safety I did. He only hungered for her.

Korrina stilled the delicious movements she was making. "Oswin, are you going to participate?"

Shit. I'd been so preoccupied with keeping my wolf tamed, I had virtually shut down. Unclenching my hands from the sides of the chair, I groaned, "I'm sorry. My wolf is starving for you."

"Let him out a bit," she suggested, playing devil's advocate. "You're so uptight like this."

"You don't know what you're asking for, Korrina. I can't control myself in the same way."

She nipped at my mouth. "I know exactly what I'm asking for."

"Korrina," I growled out, my voice inarticulate with restraint. "You need to…"

Picking up the pace, she asked, "What do I need to do, Oswin?"

I captured her stare with hungry yellow eyes. "Run."

She hesitated too long. I caught her only a few feet away, taking her down like prey. Snarling, I plunged my teeth and cock deep into her and held her down with my weight. She screamed at the intrusion but didn't struggle. This was what she wanted—me inside her, holding nothing back.

I pounded into her over and over, not caring about the cries echoing off the bare walls of the kitchen or the frenzied knocking on the front door. My wolf didn't care. Nothing made any sense to him but fucking his mate until he came inside her, which is exactly what he did.

Laughing shakily, Korrina pushed herself up to her hands and knees when I collapsed next to her. "That … was fucking amazing," she said.

"That," I panted, "is an understatement."

"Gee, I think there might be someone here," Korrina said, as the constant knocking on the door finally turned into pounding.

I grabbed my pants and gave her a sharp slap on the ass. "You stay right here. I'm not done with you."

"You say that like it's a choice," she said, dropping back onto the floor.

Leaving my insatiable mate waiting for me, I chuckled as I zipped up my jeans and made my way to the front of the house.

The smell of jealousy and outrage coming from the wolves on the front porch stung my nose and irritated my senses, wiping the smile from my face as soon as I opened the door. I nodded to the six wolves that were waiting outside. Everyone looked angry enough to spit nails. "Morning, what can I help you gentle-males with?"

My second, Thom, spoke up. "It ain't right, what you're doing to that female in there."

Korrina chose that moment to join us wearing nothing but a smile. If her body could accommodate it, she would have me inside her right now. There was no denying it. Everyone here could scent her arousal. I smirked. "You can ask my mate. I'm not doing anything she hasn't asked for."

Thom harrumphed. "Not likely. Fuck her to death for all I care. Maybe then, you'll mate with a wolf like you're supposed to."

"Every one of you could smell her desire last night!" I snapped. "Did any of the females of the pack ever smell like that for me?" I gave Thom's mate of twenty-five years an appreciative glance and continued. "Thom, just because your appetites stray from your own plentiful bounty doesn't mean mine do. I mated Korrina because she was made for me. Is that not why you mated Garnet?"

Thom's face was livid. "How dare you bring my mate into this!"

"How dare I?" I retorted. "How dare you? I've been disgraced at my mating, interrupted on my mating night, and now you are abusing my mate. Have you no shame?"

"No, Oswin, I don't. I'm a wolf, not a human, and when I'm Alpha, I'll finally be able to act like one again."

I couldn't believe my ears. He was no match for me. A fight between us would be a death sentence for him. "Are you challenging me, Thom?"

He started walking to his truck. "Nope, no one could beat you in a fair fight. I suggest you watch your back. Your guards won't always be there for you."

"You can't be Alpha if you kill me with treachery. You know that, Thom."

He turned around and smiled a wide, toothless grin. "Spoken like a true human. What does any of that matter to a wolf?"

"You're all insane!" I roared, disgusted at their behavior. They ignored me, climbed in their vehicles, and drove away. "I have to make some calls, Korrina. Can you get showered and meet me in the living room for a security debriefing in twenty minutes?"

"Sure." She sighed. "This all turned to shit quickly, didn't it?"

Truer words were never spoken.

YOU'RE THE BOMB

KORRINA

October 28th

I'm scared, journal. Really scared.

Oswin won't listen to me. He keeps assuring me that we're safe. I know how far from the truth that is. But how do you convince an Alpha to leave his own pack-lands in the middle of a turf war? It's impossible. Territory is everything to a wolf.

The only thing is ... things can only escalate from here.

And they will. I'm sure of it.

K

Less than forty-eight hours into our mating, I no longer felt safe on the pack-lands. What had been a calm and serene setting for our ceremony was now a focal point for an oncoming mutiny. It was a nightmare. Every hour, Oswin had to multiply the guard to offset the increasing number of wolves surrounding the house.

Through the back bedroom window, I listened as a giant oak relayed its latest report. The trees outside the house had been a great help, telling us what to expect from the wolves and when to expect it. Thom had been successful in infecting the pack with his anarchic obsession, but he apparently wasn't smart enough to know nymphs could communicate with trees, trees that they were spilling all their plans to without even realizing it.

Making my way to the kitchen, I plopped down in a chair and said, "Oswin, I need to spend a little time outside. I'm feeling cooped up."

He hung up the phone and nodded, almost to himself. He'd been on his cell, talking almost continuously since our unwelcome company showed up. "I'll have the guards take you outside when some of the wolves leave for the eve…"

I held up my hand to stop him, listening intently to the oak's newest warning. "They're not going to leave. The trees tell me Thom has been telling the pack that you're taking your allies and creating an elite, human-tolerant pack here on the pack-lands. He told them you're going to make them leave their homes if they don't fall in line."

Naturally, Oswin became upset. "They believe me capable of that? After all I've done for them? I saved them from themselves. And this is the thanks I get?"

"I'm so sorry about all this, Oswin."

He joined me at the table and put his arms around me from behind. "You have nothing to be sorry for. You haven't broken any of our rules, not like the wolves out there have. Their righteousness has blinded them." He sighed with the weight of the world on his shoulders. "If anyone is to blame, it's me. I fooled myself into believing the wolves could be saved when I should have just left them to their depravity and found another pack."

I stood and let him wrap me in his strong arms. "Don't you dare blame yourself. Blame those traitorous jackasses out there. You should hear some of the things they're saying about you right now."

He chuckled. "Having the trees on our side makes reconnaissance much easier."

I laughed. "In my experience, it does. Just don't ask them for a solution. You should hear the suggestions they're making on how to 'fix' the problem. All of them involve murder."

His golden brows shot up in surprise. "Whoa. I didn't expect trees to be so bloodthirsty."

I shrugged. "Yeah, well, they've watched this pack go downhill for a long time, which is why they're coming up with an escape plan for us."

"Escape? If you need to leave the house, you can get the guards to take you."

"I'm just going to stop you there. I really don't want to have to go through some epic saga every time I run to the drugstore. They have to go … or we do."

He kissed my forehead. "I told you you'd learn to hate them."

"So you did," I replied bitterly.

His cell phone rang a half a ring before he shoved it next to his ear. "Solon, how are you? Yes, of course. Hold on a moment." He handed me the phone and left me in privacy.

"Hello?"

"The trees are circulating news of a possible change in pack leaders," my uncle told me. "I take it the wolves aren't satisfied with Oswin's choice of mate?"

"I wish it was only that. One of them is spreading lies about Oswin throughout the pack. He's gaining supporters."

"Have you seen any change in the pack's behavior?" he asked in a very familiar, clinical voice.

I smiled to myself. My uncle, the invariable scholar. He was always looking to learn something new. "You could say that. There's about twenty of them having a sit-in on the front lawn."

"I thought there might be some backlash, but not to that extent and definitely not this soon after the ceremony."

I guess it was time to fess up. He should know every angle if he was going to try to help us, and I really hoped he would. "I may have changed my vows at the last minute during the ceremony."

"I bet that upset some of them. Wolves are a very traditional race."

"It did."

"What is your mate going to do about this … revolution?"

"I have no idea. I'll put him on." I was kind of interested to know what he intended to do myself.

I handed the phone to Oswin, who started laying out a game plan as soon as the phone reached his lips. My mouth dropped open. This whole time I thought he was underestimating the pack, but really, I was underestimating him.

After telling Solon that he'd send him an email, he abruptly hung up, tapped the screen a few times, and said, "Pack your things. I'm getting you out of here. Solon is only ten minutes away."

"Where are we going?"

"You're going to Meadowbrook. I'm staying here."

"You're kicking me out?" Surely, he didn't intend to try to make the wolves see reason. They said themselves their issues weren't only with me.

"I can assure you that nothing makes me as unhappy as you having to leave our home, Korrina. You're my mate."

"Then why am I leaving? It won't solve anything. You know that."

He wiped a tear off my cheek with his thumb. "Maybe without you here, they will see more clearly and start to reconsider their hostility toward our mating and the changes I've implemented in the pack."

He said all of this with a perfectly straight face. I, on the other hand, exploded. "Are you out of your fucking mind? There's no way that Thom is going to do that. They want you gone. Do you really think they won't kill you the first chance they get?"

"They might, but I have to try to turn this pack around before it's too late."

I looped my arm in his and pulled him to the front window. "Look outside, Oswin. It's too late."

"This pack has been here for four hundred years, Korrina." There was a note of hysteria in his voice. "It can't end with me.

Not like this. Can you understand that?"

I stroked a hand down his stubbled cheek. "I understand desperation. I truly do. But I also understand that some battles cannot be won." I motioned toward the window. "This one can't be won, Oswin. And I know you mean to save me by sending me away, but you can't communicate with nature as I can. I'm an asset that you can't afford to lose if you intend to fight."

He moved me away from the window. "Darlin', I hope it never comes to that."

"Get down!" the trees screamed in my head. "He's got a bomb!"

"DOWN!" I screamed, barely getting the word out before an explosion rocked the house. Oswin, directly in the line of fire, was hit hard by the crumbling wall and knocked unconscious.

"Someone, please help me!" I cried out in complete despair, knowing full well there were no willing wolves left to help.

But there were trees.

The great oak's limbs crashed through the gaping hole in the roof, raining debris on top of us. "Hurry child," it said. "Before they see you. You are not safe here, and your wolf needs medical attention I cannot provide."

Scrambling up from my knees, I ran toward the smaller limbs and branches that were lifting Oswin and followed them as they worked to move his limp body to the center of the tree. In my panic, the process seemed to take hours, but in reality, the trees had acted so fast, the dust hadn't even had time to settle yet.

Upright again and seemingly innocuous, the oak spoke silently. "Your kin is just outside the boundary. You need to make your escape while the wolves are searching the house."

"What about Oswin?" I whispered. I didn't want him to wake up forty feet from the ground with no idea what had happened. "What if he wakes up?"

"I will speak to the wolf when he awakens. Now, hurry. The trees will keep you safe. Travel along the tops, and you will slip by unseen."

"Thank you. You saved our lives," I said, my eyes welling up with tears.

"There will be plenty of time for those sentiments later. Go to your kin. He is waiting."

I kissed Oswin's bruised face and jumped up on to the oak's waiting branches. Stealthily climbing out, I leaped from limb to limb, skimming over the tops of the trees without even the slightest hesitation, and soon, I saw Solon's Toyota waiting for me on the side of the highway. I slid down a pine tree at full speed and ran for his car like I was on fire.

Once inside, I became hysterical. "Go! We have to get help!" I yelled.

Solon did as he was told, fishtailing before gaining control then tearing down the interstate. "What happened? Where's Oswin?" he asked, not taking his eyes from the road in front of him.

"He's hurt. I don't know how badly. They bombed the house. He was unconscious when I left him."

"You left him in the house? Is he well hidden?" He looked over to me, his eyes widening. "Korrina! Are you okay?"

Tears filled my eyes. "I'm fine. Oswin should be fine, too. The great oak behind the house is hiding him far from the ground. No one will find him up there."

Solon pursed his lips. "It's not at all like them to get involved in the affairs of others. You must be a good friend."

"Not really. I think the trees are in agreement with Oswin's stance. They know evil when they see it. And Solon, these wolves are truly evil."

"Korrina, I believe Oswin anticipated something like this

would happen. The email he sent me a few minutes ago had some particular requests if he were ever to be incapacitated or killed."

"He thought he might be killed?" I asked, unable to understand his reasoning for not clueing me in to the danger he was expecting. "What did the email say?"

"To fetch Obsidian."

I stopped wiping at the plaster dust on my cheeks. "Excuse me?"

He turned off on the next exit. "We're going to spring Obsidian."

Stunned, I asked, "Are we breaking him out of the Bureau?"

"No. The Alpha Female of the Thomasville pack is picking up her consort."

"My ... consort?"

Solon smiled. "It's well documented that wolves can have only one mate, but what's not as well documented is the fact that wolves can have as many consorts as they like. You, being the Alpha female, can bestow diplomatic immunity on any or all of your consorts."

"Oh, thank God," I said, sighing in relief.

"Yes. Do you think we should stop for some food? Obsidian may be hungry when he gets out."

I didn't answer him. My mind was racing with questions. "Why didn't Oswin tell me about this loophole? We could have freed him right after the mating."

Solon gave me a sage look. "My dear, your feelings for Obsidian have always been rather transparent in the past, and to top it off, you're a nymph. He is not blind to this. If you were Oswin, would you parade the fact that your mate could have sex with any male she chooses?"

I blushed, embarrassed, and shook my head. That one, I think I might keep under my hat. "I guess you're right, and you know, I'm actually relieved he didn't tell me. What else don't I know?"

"There's so much more, but I'm not the one who should be saying it. Let's just take this one step at a time, okay?"

"Okay." I sat back in my seat in overload. Getaway car driving uncles, springing consorts from prison, and a severely injured mate? This couldn't be my life. Checking groceries and picking my little sisters up from school was the highlight of my day only a month ago.

Solon picked up his cell from the dash and spoke. "The Bureau."

My eyes bugged out. He had the Bureau on speed dial? My uncle was just full of unanticipated surprises. "What are you doing?" I whispered.

"Shhhh…" he said, holding a hand up. "Hello, this is Mr. Raines' attorney. Yes, the vampire. Yes, vampires have lawyers." He cleared his throat. "The reason for my call is to inform you that the delegates from the Thomasville pack are going to arrive within the next hour to collect him. He will be released immediately in accordance with section 2266 of the Were Bill of Rights. Yes, I'm perfectly serious. We shall arrive momentarily." He hung up the phone and shook his head in disgust. "They're morons … every single one of them."

I'd never heard Solon talk like that. Really, I'd never seen him so … unchained. He was a judge, and he acted like a judge. "Are you okay?"

He sighed. "I'll be better once Obsidian is in this car with us and we've rescued your mate. Alpha wolf or not, he's family now."

I laughed. "Such a prestigious honor."

He cringed. "Yeah, I heard about your parents' visit. Honestly, I'm not sure I'm really related to your mother."

"I have my doubts, too," I said seriously. "So, is getting Obsidian released really going to be as easy as your making it out to be?"

"It should be. It only took Oswin three minutes to have you out the door."

"Good," I said. It was time to make things right. Well, one thing right.

The Bureau was just as scary on the outside as it was in the inside. Gray concrete walls topped with barbed wire and silver spikes surrounded the already heavily protected complex. The birds happily chirping from the trees above did nothing to help the atmosphere.

Solon grasped my trembling hand. "Be confident. You are well within your right to do this."

"I can do this," I said, more to myself than him.

He squeezed my hand. "Yes, you can. I'll be right behind you every step of the way."

Solon and I got out of the car and walked to the front gate. A male in what looked like a glass-enclosed closet stopped us on the way in. "State your business," he said, sounding bored.

I gave him a haughty glance. "I'm here to retrieve my consort, Obsidian Raines. I'm the Alpha female of the Thomasville pack, and this man," I said, motioning to Solon, "is attorney to both of us."

He straightened immediately. "Yes, Ma'am. Y'all come on through the gate."

I inclined my head regally. "Thank you."

Solon whispered in my ear. "I told you. Just act confident."

The guard from the gate took us all the way to the front desk. "They're here for the vampire."

The siren at the desk gave us a disgusted look and shoved the release papers at us. "Sign." She turned to her co-worker. "Go get the vampire, Jones."

Jones left his desk but came back empty handed mere moments later. "He's being uncooperative. You'll have to get him yourself."

Solon huffed, shocked at their behavior, but me? I'd play. I wanted Obsidian out of that silver hell now. "Fine." I pushed my way past the guards and strode down the hallway, calling out his name.

His weak reply came from the first door on my left. "I'm here."

"Get your ass over here and unlock the door," I told the guard. "He sounds pretty cooperative to me."

Obsidian darted out of the cell as soon as the door was open and pulled me to his side. "Let's go."

We were met with Solon's relieved face in the lobby. "All right, you two lovebirds ready to go?" he asked. "I've taken care of the paperwork."

I grinned, unable to contain my giddiness. "Thank you, Judge Manetas. We are."

***

Once we were back on the highway, Solon started mumbling to himself. Not his usual 'I can't find my document' mumbling. No, this was honest to God talking to himself, complete with fervid glances in the rearview mirror.

"What's going on up there?" I asked him.

His eyes met mine in the mirror. "Obsidian ... how's he doing?"

Obsidian groaned. "It's not going too good, old friend."

Solon turned on his blinker. "I'm going to find a human for you to feed on."

"What?" I squeaked out, shocked at his words. "Are you

serious? You can't do that! What if he kills them?"

"Better them than you," he said, his voice resolute.

"How could you say that?" I demanded. "You're a judge. And I'm immortal."

"You're my niece. They are not."

Our argument came to a screeching stop when Obsidian launched himself on top of me and bit deep into my neck. The bite was rough, his grasp on my arms tight, but I could tell he was being as gentle as a starving vampire could be.

Solon slammed on the brakes, and we screeched to a stop on the shoulder. "Korrina! Are you okay?"

I gave him two thumbs up. With my nymph metabolism, I would be back to normal in twenty minutes.

Solon sighed. "This has been the single most insane evening of my life."

Obsidian loosened his grip, finally sated. "Sorry," he said sleepily against my shoulder.

"I'm fine," I assured him.

"Are you sure?" Solon asked, handing a handkerchief to me. "You're bleeding pretty badly."

"By the time we make it back to Thomasville, we'll both feel much better." I pushed the hair off Obsidian's forehead and wiped the blood from his mouth. "This isn't the first time I've fed him." I left the "or the last time" unsaid.

A KISS GOODBYE

OBSIDIAN

I couldn't tell if she was real. She tasted real, smelled real. Had Korrina really gotten me out of that silver torture chamber?

I reached up and touched her porcelain skin. "Korrina?" She held my hand to her cheek and smiled. Was I in her lap? I sprang upright and took in my surroundings. "Where are we?"

"In Solon's car. I named you my consort to get you out of the Bureau."

"You can do that?" I asked.

"We just did," she said, with a laugh that was music to my ears.

"Where is Oswin?" Wouldn't he have accompanied Korrina to do something like this?

Korrina hiccupped, a tear slipping down her cheek.

"He's not …"

"No," Solon said. "Not yet."

"I had to leave him," Korrina sobbed. "He was knocked unconscious when we were attacked by the pack. An oak tree behind his house helped us escape. He's hiding Oswin until we can get him out of there."

I shook my head in wonder. "I can't believe this. I get locked up for a couple days, and you're already in trouble with a wolf pack?"

She smacked me on the arm. "Will you help us or not?"

"Yes, my love," I assured her, kissing the top of her head. If Oswin managed to let go of his pride long enough to tell them how I could be freed, he really did need my help. With our history, he would have only done it as a last resort.

Three miles from the pack-lands, I sent a reluctant Solon away for his safety then turned Korrina and me into mist. Within ten minutes, we arrived at what was left of Oswin's small house. It was eerily quiet, and in complete shambles, the roof was torn off by what looked like a giant hand, or in this case, a giant tree. Korrina shook her head at the mess while she reoriented herself to being solid again then gasped so loud, I had to hold my hand over her mouth.

"The oak, Obsidian," she whispered, pointing at a crater in the ground. "It's gone!"

I spun her to face me. "We don't know he's dead yet. That may have been for revenge. We need to find where their hideout is. If he's alive, he'll be there."

She nodded mutely, numb from the pain. I knew the feeling she was experiencing. I'd felt it myself when Edith died.

Wrapping her in my arms, I dematerialized and went in search of Oswin's traitorous wolves. Outside the house, everything was silent, unmoving. The pack-lands were a ghost town. There was nothing, no one left.

"Where are they?" Korrina demanded when we took form just beyond the boundaries. She was distraught. Her movements were jerky and erratic, almost as if she was drugged.

"Ask the trees," I told her gently. "They probably saw everything."

She nodded and went to the nearest pine. Laying her hands on it, she asked, "Do you know where the Alpha is?"

Instantly, the tree went from still to trembling. Her face grew pale. "He is west," she said, "near where the dry creek splits in two. Patricia and Thom want us to think he's dead. They believe they will remain within pack law if Thom defeats me for the title of Alpha this way."

"I know where that is," I said, gritting my teeth. They would never touch my Korrina. I would kill them all myself before they laid a hand on her.

Dematerializing, I zipped us through the forest, finding what was left of the pack exactly where the tree had indicated they would be. The dilapidated buildings they were using as an outpost looked barely able to withstand a strong gust of wind, much less the strength of an Alpha werewolf. The holding cell Oswin was in was downright pathetic. He could have easily broken his way out if he desired it. He must have been waiting on Korrina to return with me, just in case he was overwhelmed.

Hurriedly misting through a shattered pane of glass, we became substantial once we were directly behind the chair he was tied to. I started snapping the cable ties they used to bind his hands and feet. "The cavalry has arrived," I told him.

"Took you long enough," he mumbled through his gag.

At this, Korrina dove onto Oswin, first removing the dirty rag from his mouth then kissing every inch of his face. Tears were streaming down her cheeks. "I thought you were dead, you idiot wolf."

He put a consoling arm around her, letting her snuggle into his side for comfort. "Not yet, darlin'," he murmured, as he kissed the top of her head. "Not before I kill those fucking traitors."

I straightened and tried to ignore the love of my life as she burrowed a hole in my nemesis' side. After all the shit I'd been through because of him, he still got her? How fucking unfair was that?

Oswin looked over and finally acknowledged me. "Thanks for coming, brother."

"As if I could say no to her. She was hysterical," I shot back, wanting to rip his fucking hands off Korrina's body. How could I have ever thought her being with him was a better alternative than me? Look what had happened since he came into her life. "Let's just get her out of here."

He passed Korrina to me. "I need to take care of some things first. Do your disappearing act and meet me outside?"

Korrina slid her hands around my waist. "Hurry, Oswin."

I turned us to mist, but I couldn't leave as Oswin asked. He wasn't out of trouble yet. I didn't want his arrogance to cost him his life. His mate would never forgive me.

We watched as Oswin tied the gag around his mouth and let out a strangled howl.

A minute later, a scruffy-faced blond wolf walked in with a smirk. "What do you want, Alpha?

"Water," Oswin croaked.

The wolf laughed and headed back the way he'd come. "Sure, I'll just fetch that for you, shall I?"

Oswin leaped out of the chair, catching the unsuspecting traitor's neck with a massive paw. The wolf yelped and tried to get away, but Oswin was beyond forgiveness. He grabbed his head and beat it against the cell's bars until he didn't even twitch anymore. Blood-splattered and panting, Oswin continued on his way, leaving a trail of mangled bodies in his wake. He was focused in a way that I'd never seen before. His actions were almost mechanical. He killed a wolf, male or female, then left their broken body behind him without a second glance, moving on to the next one.

I moved us outside when Korrina's horrified emotions washed over me like a wave. She'd seen enough. Oswin was more than capable of taking care of himself. Scanning the area for wolves, I found the area strangely absent of living creatures. No birds, squirrels, or deer—none at all. I couldn't hear even the tiniest heartbeat. Had Oswin scared off everything with his rampage inside?

"We have to go!" Korrina screamed in my head. "The trees are planning retaliation for the great oak's death. Get to Oswin—now!" Still listening to the trees, she continued, "They thank Oswin for the sacrifice of his brothers and sisters, but no wolves will be allowed to return here after today."

Oswin emerged from the building covered in blood, just as we materialized. His gaze ricocheted around the dry creek bed in front of us. "What's going on? Where is … everything?"

"Getting the hell out of Dodge," I told him. "The trees are going to take care of your little traitor problem in retaliation for the great oak's death."

His face was incredulous. "What? Are you serious?"

"Yeah," I told him, lifting Korrina into my arms. "And they said, 'Thanks for your help, but get the fuck out, and don't come back'."

Oswin looked to Korrina for clarification but didn't get any. In complete shock, she was staring at him like she didn't know him anymore. He sighed. "My truck is about a mile out."

We ran, the cracking and groaning sounds of the trees awakening to exact their revenge loud in our ears. It took everything I had in me not to speed ahead and leave Oswin to whatever fate awaited him.

At his truck, Oswin slammed the key in the lock on his driver's side, got in, and reached over to open our door. "Look out!" he screamed, staring behind us.

I didn't have time to react. Before I could turn, I was slung, face first, in the mud beside the truck. I struck out behind me in case my attacker planned on staking me while I was down, but no one was there. Fearing the worst, I darted back up and turned to see my Korrina, my everything, with a knife buried in her chest and a female wolf howling in victory above her prone form.

My bellow of rage was drowned out by a deafening crack that made everyone look up.

Lightning quick, the she-wolf was impaled and pinned to the ground by a pine limb through her heart. The world was silent after that, the only noise the fading beat of my lover's heart.

With my only chance at vengeance stolen, I looked down to the beloved creature that had been taken from me. No. This couldn't happen to her. I wouldn't allow it. She would live.

Oswin's solemn howl rang in my ears as I gently picked her up and started to run.

A NEW BEGINNING

There was a sweetness on my lips, like the most delicious nectar. I licked at it and felt comforting warmth in my belly. More nectar was given. I greedily lapped it up. I was so hungry.

"Do you want more, Korrina? You must be starving," Obsidian's voice said.

"I am," I croaked out, my voice gravelly like a chain-smoker's. I squinted at his shape over me, blinking at the brightness from the lights. My vision was so blurred I couldn't make him out.

"Don't open your eyes yet. You're going to need a couple minutes to adjust."

"Okay," I said, accepting more of the nectar, then I drifted off to sleep.

***

I woke to loud, angry voices. Feigning sleep, I listened to the argument going on over me.

"She's changed," Oswin said. The close proximity of his gruff voice made me realize that he was rubbing my fingers as if they were cold, but I was toasty warm, not cool at all.

"How has she changed?" Obsidian's voice replied. "She's only said a couple of words and slept."

"She looks different, smells different—even feels different. She's changed."

"So?"

"So, she used to remind me of the spring. She smelled earthy and wild. Now there's nothing but a corpse."

"That's your mate you're talking about, wolf. How do you think she'd feel if she heard you say things like that?"

194

"I know it would hurt her. Damn it! I don't want to hurt her! She saved my life."

"Is that the only reason why? Why did you even mate her if you don't love her? Was it just to take her away from me?"

When Oswin didn't answer, I forced my eyes open. I'd had enough.

Obsidian raced to my side. "Are you hungry?" He offered a bloodied, mangled wrist.

"Get that the hell out of here! Gross!" I shrieked, kicking the blankets off of me and pushing myself up into a sitting position.

To my left, Oswin's heartbeat quickened. Had I always been able to hear his heartbeat? I couldn't remember. My memories of him were hazy, a lifetime ago.

"Oswin?"

He stiffened next to me. "Darlin'?"

"Your heart is beating so fast. What's wrong?"

He didn't answer, just kept his eyes on the door out of the room, like he was calculating whether he could make it to there before I did.

"Don't," I said to him. He didn't listen, just kept walking. Confused, I threw my legs over the edge of the bed to stand up. The next thing I knew, I was in front of him. I shoved him into the chair in the corner with unnatural strength when he crashed into me. "Why are you running away from me, Oswin?"

"I don't want to hurt you," he growled.

With my unfocused vision, I could only make out the color of Oswin's yellow wolf eyes, but not his expression. "Someone please tell me what's going on. Why am I holding my mate down?" I asked, pushing him back into the chair when he tried to stand.

Obsidian pulled me away from Oswin and led me to the foot of the bed to sit. "I believe you owe her more of an explanation, wolf."

He grudgingly nodded and met my eyes, which were starting to clear. "Korrina …"

Just the crack in Oswin's voice told me our mating was no more. It was over. The tears I'd been holding back ran over my cheeks, dotting my shirt with tiny bloody circles. I jerked my hand to the pulse in my wrist. "Obsidian, no."

"I couldn't let you die," he said. "I'm so sorry."

Like the snap of a rubber band, everything shot back into place. I ripped open my shirt, looking for the stab wound. It was gone, smoothed over like it was never there. "I'm a …?" I put my fingers in my mouth and felt around. "There's nothing here."

Obsidian smiled patiently. "Who do you think did this to my arm? They'll come back out when you want them to."

I stared at his mutilated wrist and started to get angry. "Is Patricia dead?"

Oswin finally spoke, albeit bitterly. "A tree took care of her right after you were stabbed. If it had been just one second earlier, it would have saved you from becoming what you are."

"What I am?" I snapped. "I'm still me, Oswin."

"You're nothing like yourself," he yelled back. "You're a corpse. You have no heartbeat. You drink blood. You're not the female I mated."

His words bore a hole in my chest. He didn't want me anymore? Had he ever? I stared at the moonlight shining brightly through the window pane and asked, "Why did you mate me, Oswin? Did you even love me?"

"I do love you, Korrina. Maybe not in the way I'm supposed to, but I do."

"Come clean to her!" Obsidian hissed.

"Korrina, please believe that I never meant to hurt you. I only ever intended to stop Obsidian from finding happiness with you.

I've been angry over Edith for so long, torturing him became a way of life for me. I honestly didn't think that I would feel the way I did for you. It took me by surprise."

"Edith? Obsidian's wife? What does she have to do with this?"

Oswin sighed. "She was my sister. When she took up with Obsidian, it destroyed my parents. It made them crazy. I just wanted to punish him for what he put my family through. Why should he have happiness when we were so miserable?"

"But you said that you challenged your father over her death. If you were angry enough about it to kill your father, why would you keep torturing Obsidian?

"I've hated him for sixty years, Korrina. If he hadn't followed my sister into that alley, she and my parents would be with me today."

"How could you possibly know that?" I asked, starting to pace.

Oswin looked to Obsidian, who got up and put his hands on my shoulders. "Calm down, Korrina. There's no need to get upset."

I gave him a withering look. "Oh, I'm sorry, Oswin. Please continue breaking my black, vampire heart. Wouldn't you like to tell me all about how you mated me just to keep your title? Or maybe, we can talk about how I don't smell like spring anymore?"

Oswin sidled toward the door. "I'm going to go. I'm so sorry, Korrina."

Screaming through gritted teeth, I was ready to rip his throat out to alleviate this hurt. This was his fault—the mating, our incarceration, my vampirism—everything.

"Just let him go, Korrina," Obsidian pleaded with me, still tightly gripping my shoulders.

I couldn't. All I could think about was revenge, of hurting him as much as he'd hurt me.

Breaking free of his grasp, I dove headfirst out of his bedroom window. I hit the ground running and caught Oswin just as he was getting into his truck. "Going somewhere?" I hissed, grabbing his collar and slinging him into the grass. In a blur, I straddled him and bit savagely into his neck, letting the blood flow over my mouth until it painted the ground below him red.

"Korrina! Stop!" Obsidian bellowed from the window loud enough to wake the dead.

Stop? Was he kidding? If there were ever an insurmountable task, that would be stopping. God, his blood was good. Not as good as Obsidian's, but it was damn close.

With a surge of life-saving strength, Oswin pushed me off of him and tried to climb into the safety of his truck. I almost decided to let him go—almost.

"Korrina! Let him go!"

Obsidian's angry voice pierced through the haze of my bloodlust. I looked at Oswin's mangled neck in my hands and gagged. I was so embarrassed, so horrified by what I'd done, I ran.

Even when Obsidian screamed for me to come back, I didn't stop, just pushed forward as fast as my legs would carry me until I was sure I'd lost him. I collapsed atop the knotty roots of a water oak after a few miles, too emotionally exhausted to carry on.

"Thank God!" I cried out, sobbing in relief when she acknowledged me. If I still had my connection to the trees, I was still me, not just a vampire.

"You are changed, child."

"Cursed," I hiccupped, weeping into my hands.

"Why do you weep? You have sacrificed all for the wolf, and still, he rejects you. Do not despair his loss. You are now a mirror image of the one who has always truly loved you. That cannot be a curse."

Before I could respond, Obsidian took form ten feet away, holding up his arms in a universal 'I'm not going to hurt you' way. His voice was low, hypnotizing when he spoke. "Come to me, Korrina."

I leaped into his arms, crushing my body to his, my mind spinning wildly from Oswin's blood. "I'm so sorry. I didn't mean to hurt him."

He pushed my hair from my face. "It's okay, my love. You're very new to this change. No one would expect you to be perfect so soon after your transformation."

I nodded, looking up at the lightening sky on the horizon. I could feel the heat, though it wasn't even dawn yet. "Can you take us back to the house, Obsidian? I'm scared."

He wiped the blood from my lips with his thumb and gently kissed me. "My pleasure, love."

Back inside the house, Obsidian carried me into his bedroom, stripped me of my bloody clothes, and laid me on the bed. "Relax, my love. Sleep, if you can. When you wake up, we will talk about everything that's happened. We have all the time in the world to figure this mess out."

I reached for his retreating form. "Please don't leave me. I don't want to be alone."

"I'll never leave you," he said, stretching out next to me. His strange amber eyes were burning with emotion.

"I love you, Obsidian," I said, kissing his lips slowly, softly, until his fangs emerged.

His smile was wicked as he lifted himself on top of me, his erection hard and searching. "I love you more, Korrina."

Instantly distracted, I unzipped his pants to find his velvety hardness and stroked him. "Prove it."

Without a second thought, he tore the crotch out of my panties and thrust his hard sex into me, groaning with pleasure. "Marry me, Korrina," he said. It wasn't a question. It was a demand.

"Yes," I answered, holding tightly to him as I moaned in my indulgence. Sex had never felt like this before. There was no doubt he had been holding back the intensity he was capable of until I had strength like his. "Always."

Crushing his mouth to mine, he kissed me until my lips were bruised and swollen and my body was aching with need. "Korrina, I would have waited an eternity for you."

THE END

Books by J.D. Nelson

Wicked Ways Series

A Night of Wickedness
*All I Want For Christmas Are My Two Front Fangs: A Wicked
Ways Companion Novel*
Wolves Will Be Wolves
Too Cute To Spook: A Wicked Ways Companion Novel

Night Aberrations Series

Night Aberrations
The Fire within the Night

Tales of Desire

Control

Havenwood Falls Sin & Silk Novellas

Plans Laid Bare
Soul Laid Bare

About the Author

JD Nelson is a Bestselling Author of Fantasy Romance and Adult Paranormal Romance. An avid time-waster, JD enjoys watching TV and listening to audiobooks when she really should be writing. JD loves to hear from her readers. You can contact her through her website, AuthorJDNelson.com, or on Facebook, where she spends an alarming amount of time chatting with her many Author and reader friends, much to the dismay of her continually neglected manuscripts.

JD Nelson's Facebook
www.facebook.com/NightAberrations
JD Nelson's Twitter
https://twitter.com/authorjdnelson
JD Nelson's Facebook Fan Page
www.facebook.com/JDNelsonsNightAberrations
JD Nelson's Fan Club
http://www.facebook.com/groups/269730583130725/

www.ingramcontent.com/pod-product-compliance
Lightning Source LLC
Chambersburg PA
CBHW060216180626
46813CB00007B/2847